'Why didn't you say something?'

Jack smiled slowly. 'Such as?'

'Well—I don't know—anything! "I'm your new boss" would have done nicely. You just stood there and made a complete fool of me——'

He shook his head. 'Oh, no, Irish, you did that all by yourself.'

Kathleen blushed again. 'You could have said something,' she repeated stubbornly.

He shrugged and grinned. 'I suppose so, but it just seemed like a bit of harmless fun—and you know, Irish, you're beautiful when you're angry.'

Dear Reader

Variety is the spice of life and that is certainly true of Caroline Anderson's book this month, set in a busy accident and emergency department. A strong book medically, and emotionally. We also have a cruise setting, a hospital librarian heroine from the Norfolk coast, and a student nurse with a real problem to solve that could affect many lives. Four books to get your teeth into—enjoy!

The Editor

Caroline Anderson's nursing career was brought to an abrupt halt by a back injury, but her interest in medical things led her to work first as a medical secretary, and then after completing her teacher training, as a lecturer in medical office practice to trainee medical secretaries. In addition to writing, she also runs her own business from her home in rural Suffolk, where she lives with her husband, two daughters, mother and dog.

Recent titles by the same author:

JUST WHAT THE DOCTOR ORDERED

THE SPICE OF LIFE

BY

CAROLINE ANDERSON

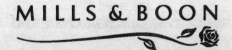

MILLS & BOON LIMITED
ETON HOUSE, 18–24 PARADISE ROAD
RICHMOND, SURREY, TW9 1SR

For Annie
who gave me the carrots in the frilly
and lots, lots more. Bless you.

First published in Great Britain 1993
by Mills & Boon Limited

© Caroline Anderson 1993

Australian copyright 1993
Philippine copyright 1993
This edition 1993

ISBN 0 263 78345 6

Set in 10 on 12 pt Linotron Times
03-9310-50844

Typeset in Great Britain by Centracet, Cambridge
Made and printed in Great Britain

CHAPTER ONE

KATHLEEN HENNESSY was spoiling for a fight.

She had just spent a weekend at home in Belfast dutifully admiring the latest Hennessy grandchild and enduring countless little digs about good Catholic girls and settling down to raise a family instead of racketing about the world enjoying herself — as if it was such a sin to enjoy life, for God's sake, she thought angrily, and anyway six years as Sister in the accident and emergency department of the Audley Memorial in Suffolk hardly constituted racketing! Anybody would think she was a promiscuous little tart, the way her family reproached her for her single status. . .

All except Maria. She understood — mainly because she was only twenty-six and already had four children and another on the way. She had had such a promising career as a physio, Kathleen thought crossly, and now she was trapped at home with her children while her husband powered quietly on up the career ladder, leaving her behind.

And nothing wrong with it at all, if that was what was right for you, but it wasn't right for Maria, and it sure as eggs wasn't right for Kath!

She turned her little car precisely into a parking place in the hospital car park, climbed out and slammed the door. Damned dictators! Why couldn't they just understand that she didn't want to be married and settled with umpteen kids and a mortgage up to the sky and no life to call her own?

Selfish, they'd called her. OK. That was fine. So she was selfish. Perhaps that was why she worked the hours she did in the most gruelling part of the hospital, picking up the pieces — literally, sometimes — and putting them back together if possible, consoling distraught relatives if not.

'They probably think I'm still carrying bedpans all day!' she said to no one in particular, and locked her car door with a vicious twist.

As she did so she glanced towards the entrance of A and E, checking automatically for Jim Harris's car — except it wouldn't be there, she remembered with a twinge of regret. Jim had left, moved on to London and was heading up a new Rapid Response Unit there in connection with HEMS, the Helicopter Emergency Medical Service.

She wondered what his replacement would be like. Well, they'd find out soon, she thought, glancing at her watch, and then stared in amazement as a heavy black motorbike cruised lazily into the consultant's slot and stopped.

'Well, of all the nerve!' she muttered, and, yanking her keys out of the door, she shoved them into her bag and marched across the car park, head held high.

'Excuse me, you can't leave that there!' she said firmly, and looked him straight in the eye.

Her first mistake. Even through the streaky visor she could see that he had the most mesmerising eyes — laughing eyes — laughing at her. She looked hastily away — and found *her* eyes glued to a body that had no business being so magnetically attractive.

He was still sitting astride the bike, balancing it with his long, lean legs tautly encased in black leather. Hell, the whole man was tautly encased in black leather! His body flexed as he hauled the heavy bike up on to the centre stand, and her heart jerked and accelerated to a steady two hundred beats a minute. Well, that was what it felt like.

Ridiculous! She dragged her eyes up and watched as, unhurriedly, he stripped off his heavy gloves and laid them across the bike before lifting his helmet off and balancing it in front of him. His hair was dark, almost black, rumpled by the helmet but unruly anyway, and a heavy stubble covered his jaw, lending him a rakish and piratical air. His lips were firm and sensual — and twitching.

Ignoring the kick of her heart as she met his eyes again without the intervention of the visor, she tried again.

'You can't leave your bike here, it's the consultant's parking space! If he's needed urgently and he can't find anywhere to park, he could waste precious minutes while someone's lying dying for want of his attention!'

A dark, slender brow arched tauntingly above the laughing grey eyes. Holy Mary, he had lovely eyes! She forced herself to concentrate.

'Aren't you being rather melodramatic?' he said in a deep, cultured voice with a deceptively lazy lilt to it. It made her toes curl just listening to him, and perversely that made her even angrier.

'No, I'm not, and if you knew the first damn thing about Accident and Emergency you would know I wasn't!' she snapped.

He inclined his head in a cheeky little salute and

grinned. 'I concede to your superior knowledge, Sister,' he murmured.

Oh, that voice!

'Good,' she said, and was disgusted to notice that *her* voice was softening. She firmed it up. 'So, please move your bike.'

His lips twitched. 'I really don't think ——'

'Are you going to move it, or am I going to contact the hospital security staff and get them to move it for you?'

The smile blossomed on his lips and, lifting his hand, he coiled a lock of her hair around his finger, drawing her closer. 'You know, Irish,' he said softly, his voice like raw silk sliding over her senses, 'with a temper like that you really ought to have red hair. . .'

For a full second she was too stunned to move, but then she slapped his hand away, and, drawing herself up to her full five feet four, she glared at him furiously.

'That just about does it!' she hissed. Spinning on her heel, she stalked away with her head in the air.

In the midst of the morning rush-hour his laughter drifted after her, curling round her senses and inflaming her still further.

She marched into A and E, slapping the swing doors out of the way with the palm of her hand, and turned smartly into the cloakroom. Two nurses in there straightened away from the walls, murmured, 'Good morning, Sister,' and faded into the corridor.

Kathleen turned and studied herself in the mirror. 'Red hair, indeed!' she muttered. 'Rude man.' In fact, there was a trace of red when the sun was on it, but she didn't want to dwell on that at the moment! No, it was plain old dark brown, cut in a blunt bob at her

chin, easy to keep neat and tidy—unlike his wild tangle
that was almost black, except at the temples where it
was streaked with grey.

To match his eyes, she thought, and her own lost
focus as she remembered the strange way the colour
had seemed to change as he laughed. Like pebbles
underwater, flickering with the light.

Yuck. She'd be reciting poetry next!

Her own eyes were a muddy green, and just now
they were spitting fire, like a little cat. In fact it was a
wonder there wasn't smoke pouring out of her ears!

But, my God, he did look good in all that leather
gear. . .

She turned away from the mirror with a sound of
disgust. Imagine getting turned on by a biker! He was
probably smothered in tattoos, for heaven's sake! She
ruthlessly suppressed a little shiver of curiosity. Perhaps her family were right; maybe it was time she
settled down.

She took her frilly cap out of the locker and skewered
it to her hair with the pins, adjusting it until she was
satisfied that it was absolutely correct. Nothing got past
Sister Hennessy that wasn't correct—including That
Man!

She glanced at her watch and pulled a face. There
wasn't time to report the bike to the security staff
before hand over. She left the cloakroom and went to
her office, took the report from the night sister and
then went out of the office towards the nursing station.

However she didn't get there. One of the nurses she
had seen in the cloakroom was standing in the middle
of the corridor, flushed pink and grinning like an idiot,

while That Man lounged on one leg in all his taut leather and chatted her up.

Enraged, she marched up to them.

'I'm sorry, sir, but you aren't allowed in this area. It's staff only. Nurse, are you here for a reason?'

The girl blushed even pinker, and stood up straight. 'Oh — yes, Sister. I'm starting on A and E today.'

Kathleen eyed her up and down. 'Are you, indeed? Well, you'd better come with me. The exit's that way, sir,' she added pointedly, and then marched the nurse into the CSSD store.

'Right, young lady, there are a few things you need to know about how I run this unit, and the first is that my nurses don't loll around in the corridors indulging in idle chatter with strange men!'

'But, Sister, he asked me —'

'I don't want to know what he asked you! I've already had trouble with him today. The best thing you can do is keep out of his way until I get rid of him. Right, this place is chaotic. I want everything cleared up and sorted out before the rush starts again, all right? If you think we're getting low on anything, I want to know, please. I'll send another nurse in to help you. Here's the check list.'

And she swept out, heading for the phone again.

There was no sign of him now, thank goodness. Security said they'd send someone over right away, and she busied herself for the next few minutes with the half-dozen patients in the waiting area.

There was a nasty sprain which needed an X-ray, a query appendix for the surgical reg and a couple of cuts and other minor injuries which needed cleaning up and suturing.

Mick O'Shea, the surgical registrar on take and one of her old SHOs, breezed in as she was cleaning up one of the patients with a cut hand.

'Top o' the mornin' to you, Sister Hennessy!' he sang, cheerful as ever, and she shot him a black look.

'Good morning, Dr O'Shea,' she said repressively.

He pretended to look chastened, and inspected the cut with great care.

'Just a couple of wee stitches — sure you can manage, Sister?'

'Probably a great deal better than you,' she replied with a sugary smile, and after a reassuring word to her patient, she led Mick out into the corridor.

'Your patient's in here,' she said shortly.

Mick stopped her with a hand on her arm.

'What's eating you today?'

She gave a strained little chuckle. 'It shows?'

He grinned. 'Only to an expert in family relationships — and I know you were away for the weekend!'

Her chuckle relaxed. 'I've been home — got lots of grief about not being settled down with fourteen children — '

Mick laughed. 'Why under God do you imagine I never go home?'

They shared a commiserating smile, and Mick put his arm around her shoulders and gave her a friendly hug. 'Of course you could always marry me and blame the lack of children on my war wound — '

She spluttered with laughter. 'What war wound?'

He grinned cheekily. 'Poetic licence, m'darlin'! We'd make a lovely couple, don't you think? Can't you just see your mother in a pink floppy hat with cherries on it? How about a quick kiss to seal the pact?'

'Put me down, you lecherous old goat!' she said with a laugh, and, pushing him away, she straightend up in time to see That Man emerge from Jim's old office with Ben Bradshaw, the senior registrar.

He had obviously showered, the almost-black hair falling in damp curls over his broad forehead, and he had changed into casual trousers and a shirt. The stubble was gone, and he was even wearing a tie — well, nearly. It hung round his neck, the knot well below the open collar of his shirt, and in the vee she could see the cluster of damp curls at the base of his throat. He looked almost respectable — and very, very sexy. He was also in the wrong place again. Kathleen opened her mouth, and a lid drooped over one of those fabulous grey eyes in a wicked wink.

'We meet again,' he said with a grin.

'Morning,' Mick greeted him. 'Good weekend?'

That Man shrugged. 'Not bad — bit windy earlier. Good thermals, though.'

Thermals? As in underwear? Never! Kathleen glanced sharply up at Mick. 'Do you know him?'

Mick nodded, and Ben Bradshaw stepped into the yawning void. 'Have you met Sister Hennessy yet?' he asked.

That Man's full lips twitched. 'Yes, we have — er — spoken,' he said, and the smile won and tipped the corners of his lips, bringing an enticing little dimple to one cheek. He held out his hand. 'Jack Lawrence,' he said, and if the floor could have opened up and swallowed her she would have been delighted.

As the fiery blush mounted her cheeks, she shook his hand briefly, desperately hoping for a miracle.

Holy Mary, she thought, all these years I've been a good girl—can't you do something?

Apparently not. The floor stubbornly resisted her prayers and imprecations. Jack Lawrence released her hand and turned to Ben.

'So, how's the rest of the weekend been? Sorry I had to desert you yesterday.'

'Oh, not a problem. There wasn't anything too drastic.'

'Good. So, Sister Hennessy, how would you like to offer me a cup of coffee so we can get acquainted while these two young men carry on with their duties?'

Her mind flailed. 'I—I have somebody to suture——'

'Ben, would you? I think Sister Hennessy and I need to have a chat. We'll be in my office.'

And that was the end of that.

She followed him numbly, still praying for that elusive miracle as they went into the staff rest-room and collected two cups of coffee and then out again, back down the corridor to the consultant's room—his room.

On the way her mind ran over their conversation in the car park. One thing in particular sprang to mind. 'If you knew the first thing about Accident and Emergency——' Oh, Lord, let me be dreaming. .

He opened the door for her, closed it behind him and indicated the chair, then lounged against the window sill and grinned. 'Would you like to go first?'

Oh, sure—and say what? She almost laughed. 'Not really—I'm still trying to swallow the rest of my feet,' she confessed ruefully.

He chuckled, a wickedly delicious little chuckle that

sent a shiver down her spine. She set her coffee down before she slopped it all and met his eyes defiantly.

'Why didn't you say something?'

He smiled slowly. 'Such as?'

'Well — I don't know — anything. "I'm your new boss" would have done nicely. You just stood there and made a complete fool of me —'

He shook his head. 'Oh, no, Irish, you did that all by yourself.'

She blushed again. 'You could have said something,' she repeated stubbornly.

'Yes, I could, you're quite right. It was unkind of me. I apologise. '

She shot him a keen look, quite sure he was laughing at her, but his face was sober and his eyes were gentle now.

'You didn't look like a consultant.'

'No.'

'You should have said —'

'I should. You didn't really give me much chance —'

'Rubbish! You had every opportunity!'

He shrugged and grinned. 'I suppose so, but it just seemed like a bit of harmless fun — and you know, Irish, you're beautiful when you're angry.'

She was speechless.

The phone rang, and he reached out a long arm and hooked it up. 'Lawrence.'

He listened for a moment, a slow smile spreading over his face, and then held the phone out to her.

'Security for you — something about a motorbike in the car park. . .'

* * *

Kathleen supposed there was some comfort to be gained from knowing that nobody had ever died of humiliation. Doubtless in later years she would be glad of that, but for now she was too embarrassed to care.

It wouldn't have been so bad, of course, if it had only been him, but there was that second-year nurse whom she had accused of loitering with him in the corridor — that was going to take some fancy footwork to get out of without loss of face. Oh, well, at least she wasn't Japanese. Good job too, as there wasn't a handy sword to fall on. She didn't somehow think a stitch cutter would do the trick quite so well!

In the end she screwed up her courage, took the girl into her office and apologised. 'I made a mistake,' she admitted. 'I didn't realise who he was, and with the security problems hospitals have been having recently, you can't be too careful.'

The nurse smiled. 'I didn't know who he was, either, but he asked me where he could find you, and I told him I didn't know, and he said "Are you new too?" and then you arrived and. . .' She trailed to a halt. 'He didn't look — well — like a consultant, did he?'

Bless her, Kath thought. 'No, Nurse, he didn't, but he is.' She glanced at her name badge. 'Amy, have you done any work on Surgical?'

She nodded. 'I did some time with Sister Lovejoy last year, and I've done some orthopaedics.'

'And how did you get on?'

She nibbled her bottom lip. 'OK. I had a bit of a problem with Mr Hamilton when he first arrived — I did something rather stupid and he was furious, but the patient was OK and he was great after that. Sister Lovejoy was ever so kind to me over it.'

Kathleen groaned inwardly. That was all she needed, a nurse who made mistakes.

'Well, Amy, if you aren't sure about anything, you ask, OK? We can't afford to make mistakes down here. I think you'd better work with me for the next few days, or if I'm not here, then with one of my staff nurses. Right. Do you know what triage is?'

'Um — is that putting patients in order of priority as they come in so that you don't leave people to bleed to death because they're at the end of the queue?'

Kathleen winced and grinned. 'Sort of. You're on the right lines. It really comes into its own when there's a big emergency involving lots of people. Then the triage nurse is perhaps the most important member of the team. It's a tremendous responsibility, and challenges all your skills and training, but it also depends a lot on gut instinct. OK, now we're going to go and have a look in the waiting-room and at the notes, and do a bit of triage there. If they're all on a par, we take them on a first come, first served basis. Anyone with a suspected heart condition or serious bleeding or a major fracture or head injury comes first, though, and every time an ambulance brings someone, they get seen immediately in the trolley area.'

She took Amy down the corridor. 'Here we have the cubicles for the walking wounded or minor cases, then the trolley area for the major cases, and then the resus. room for the crisis cases. Then down here we have a couple of day beds for patients who need to rest under observation for the day following treatment but who don't really justify admission, and then over here we've got the two theatres for major suturing and cleaning up, and then down there at the end the X-ray and plaster rooms.'

Amy nodded, her eyes like saucers, and Kathleen remembered the first time she had worked in A and E.

'Don't worry, you'll be fine. I'll look after you.'

They checked the few patients in the waiting-room, and Kathleen got Amy to sort them into priority, talking through the decision-making process as she did so.

'Fine,' she said when Amy had finished. 'No problems there. But don't worry, you wouldn't be asked to do it alone yet. The triage nurse is always qualified and experienced, but it doesn't hurt you to see how it's done.'

It was, in fact, a ridiculously quiet day with a steady trickle of bits and pieces, an ideal day to find one's feet.

Unfortunately it meant that there wasn't enough for the consultant to do to keep him out of her way, and every time she turned round she almost fell over him.

'Are you checking up on me?' she demanded half way through the afternoon.

'Now, Irish, you know better than that,' he said with a cheeky grin, and left her alone for a few minutes.

Then there was a call on the red phone.

'OK,' Kathleen said. 'We've got someone coming in on a blue light, a young man who's fallen under a train. Could be an attempted suicide, we don't know. Anyway, there's considerable loss of blood, massive lower limb and pelvic damage and some chest injuries. We'll need plasma expander, and samples immediately for cross matching. Better have some O neg. sent up for immediate use as well. Right, let's move.'

They prepared the resus. room, and when all was ready they informed the patients still waiting that they might have a slight delay due to an emergency that was being brought in. There were the usual grumbles, but they faded instantly as the ambulance backed up to the entrance, doors already opening.

He was screaming, the high-pitched, nerve-grating scream of agony that always turned Kathleen's blood to stone, and the waiting-room fell into shocked silence.

They wheeled him rapidly into Resus., Kathleen snapping out instructions right, left and centre, but as they peeled back the blanket to examine him, even Kathleen after all the years she had been working in A and E was shocked at the extent of his injuries. Both his legs were severed completely, the right one mid-thigh, the left up at the hip. His head was cut and bleeding, and his jacket was torn and damaged, indicating possible chest injuries. His right arm was also lying at a funny angle and was probably dislocated or fractured.

Amy Winship took one look at him and disappeared quietly through the door, and Ben Bradshaw winced. Only Jack Lawrence appeared quite unmoved, glancing dispassionately at the damage that Kath revealed with her scissors. There was blood everywhere, more of it by the second, and nothing they did seemed to stop it. His left leg was particularly bad, the vessels refusing to co-operate. They slowed it to a steady well, but it wouldn't stop, and through it all there was the awful screaming.

'For Christ's sake get an anaesthetist down here and shut him up,' Jack Lawrence grunted, and moved to his head, checking his pupils automatically. 'Have we got any ID?'

Kathleen shook her head. 'No, nothing. The ambulance men checked his clothes.'

'Damn. We need to get his relatives in fast.'

She raised an eyebrow. 'You don't say?'

He grinned ruefully. 'Any sign of a surgeon? And we need cardiothoracic and orthopaedics, too.'

'Before or after the mortuary technician?' Ben said under his breath.

Kath glared at him, and he shrugged.

'Just being realistic, old thing.'

'Well, don't bother—and don't call me old thing. Just do your job, please. Have you stopped that bleeding yet?'

He shook his head. 'It's leaking from the abdomen— I think he needs a bit of surgical attention.'

Kath shot him a dry look. 'You guys are really sharp today, aren't you?'

Jack was inspecting the young man's chest dispassionately, watching the ragged rise and fall of the ribs as he dragged in a breath between screams, and he shook his head thoughtfully. While he ran thorough hands and eyes over his shattered body, Kathleen started cleaning up the chest area ready for the heart monitor after checking the IV line that was running in Haemacel and taking blood for cross-matching, dodging round the radiographer who had brought the portable in and was taking X-rays.

When his chest was clear, she put on the pads for the heart monitor, frowning slightly as she did so at the feel of the chest wall under her hands. As she watched his breath jerked in, and a large section of his chest wall moved in instead of out.

'Flail chest,' she said quietly, and Jack nodded, drawing her to one side.

'The lung's collapsed, I think. Probably where he was hit by the train. His pelvis is shot to hell, too, and judging by the feel of the abdomen, he's got massive haemorrhaging.'

Kath nodded. 'So why is he still alive?'

'God knows.' Their eyes met and tracked together to the heart monitor. 'He's not doing too well, is he? I think we need an echocardiograph. Can you get the cardiographer?'

Not that there's a great deal of point, Kathleen thought to herself, but we may as well go through the motions.

While she phoned the switchboard and requested that they page the cardiographer, Michael Barrington the orthopaedic SR arrived and glanced at the shattered stubs of the young man's femurs.

He swore, softly and succinctly. 'Got any X-rays yet?'

Jack nodded. 'Yes, they're just being developed.'

Michael pursed his lips. 'Done a real job on himself, hasn't he? Anyone know why?'

'No. We don't even know if it was an accident yet.'

Their eyes flicked to the monitor. Their patient was still alive but his condition was deteriorating visibly. The anaesthetist, Peter Graham, had arrived and managed to dull his pain. Now he merely lay and moaned, but at least he was no longer screaming.

Amy popped her head round the door to tell

Kathleen that they had found some ID on the track and the police had brought his parents in.

'His name's Steven Blowers. They want to see him.'

Kathleen exchanged glances with Jack, and he shook his head.

'Put them in the interview-room and give them a cup of tea. One of us will be out in a minute,' she told the young nurse. 'Oh, and Amy? Say nothing.'

Amy nodded gratefully and retreated.

The X-rays appeared and Michael ran a critical eye over them.

'Ouch. Do you want me to interpret, or is it academic?' he said quietly.

Jack's mouth lifted in a wry smile. 'Probably. We'll see what the cardiothoracic guy has to say.'

When he arrived moments later, he took one look at the X-rays and shook his head.

'You jest, of course?' he said drily. 'Look at this shadow here—probably a bulge in the heart or the aorta behind it—the kid's a goner. He'll never make the anaesthetic, and even if he did, who wants to be a bloody cripple? Oh, well, we can only fail. Let's have him up in Theatre.'

He sauntered out, whistling, and Kathleen met Michael Barrington's eyes. They were like chips of blue ice, his lips compressed into a thin line.

'Call me if you need me in Theatre—but I'd just as soon Tim Mayhew did it—I don't trust myself near that bastard.'

And he turned on his heel and stalked away, his limp almost imperceptible.

Jack raised an eyebrow. 'What's eating him?'

'He's a bloody cripple,' she said succinctly.

'What?'

'He has an artificial leg. He went to assist at a passenger train derailment last year and got trapped in the wreckage. We had to amputate part of his leg to free him.'

'Ah. . .'

Just then their patient moaned and opened his eyes. Kathleen was there instantly.

'Steven? It's all right, you're in hospital. Can you hear me?'

He licked his lips and nodded slightly. 'Messed it up, didn't I?' His voice was a mere thread. 'I thought it would be quick,' he went on painfully. 'Let me go — please, let me go. You don't know what this is all about.'

She squeezed his hand. 'Do you want to tell me?'

'Danny,' he whispered. 'My fault. . .gave Danny — HIV.'

'Oh, Christ,' someone muttered behind her. Kathleen closed her eyes. The room was a bloodbath, all of them were covered, and their patient was HIV positive.

Great. Oh, well, it had happened before, doubtless it would happen again. As far as she was aware, no one had cut themselves or pricked themselves with a needle.

Behind her she could hear Jack calmly telling every-one to go and shower and change and come back in full barrier gear.

She could see blood on Jack's cheek and on his arm above the gloves. God knows where it was on her.

Steve groaned again, and the nurse in her took over.

'Your parents are here, Steven. They're waiting to see you. Do you feel up to it?'

His mouth twisted in a bitter little smile. 'You mean I'm going to feel better?' he whispered.

It wasn't really a question. Kathleen lifted her head and met Jack's eyes pleadingly. He nodded.

It was time to be honest.

'You've got severe chest and abdominal injuries, as well as the injuries to your legs.'

'Will I die?'

She was struck by how blue his eyes were as they bored into her own — blue and clear, like the sky. What a bloody waste.

'I'm afraid it's quite likely.'

'Don't be — afraid. It's OK, really. It's what I want. . .'

His eyes flickered closed, and he licked his lips. 'Love a drink.'

'I'll get you some iced water.'

She found a nurse and sent her for it, and then held the cup and dabbed his lips with a swab dipped in the water.

'Thanks.' His voice was weaker. Kathleen didn't think they could afford to wait any longer.

She met Jack's eyes, and he nodded. 'I'll get them.'

'Thanks.'

As he moved past her, she took a clean swab and wiped his cheek.

'You could change your coat first.'

He glanced down and gave a short, humourless grunt of laughter. 'Yes, I think you're right. Put a blanket over him.'

He was only gone a minute, and when he returned,

it was with a couple in their fifties who were holding hands as if they were desperately hanging on to reality.

They were obviously shocked by his condition and lost for words, but he shocked them further with his.

'Never been what you wanted—I'm sorry. Never meant to hurt you,' he whispered.

Kathleen swallowed a lump in her throat, Ben coughed discreetly and Jack busied himself at the X-ray box.

The phone on the wall rang softly, and Kathleen answered it.

'Theatre's ready for him,' she said quietly.

Jack nodded and took a step towards Steve where he lay surrounded by his family, and then everything seemed to happen at once.

The monitor shrilled, Steve moaned, his mother gasped, and everybody leapt into action.

'Pressure's dropped right away,' Kath said quietly.

'Damn, he's arrested,' Jack muttered, and flung the covers off his chest.

Kath snatched up an airway and tipped back his head. 'Ben, come and bag him while I get the drugs.'

She handed the airbag to the registrar while Jack pressed rhythmically on the patient's sternum. 'What do you want, IV adrenalin, calcium and atropine?'

Jack nodded. 'And adrenalin into the heart. Let's not mess about.'

Someone suggested to his parents that they should leave, but no one had time to show them out.

She handed Jack the syringe with the long needle, and he slid it neatly between the ribs and into the heart while Kath injected the other drugs into the giving set in his arm.

'OK, let's check the monitor.'

They glared at the screen, willing the line to flutter into life, but the trace remained persistently flat.

'Come on, damn it!' Jack muttered and thumped his chest again. 'Now!'

Nothing.

'Try again?' Kath said quietly.

Jack let his breath out on a sigh and shook his head. 'His aorta's gone. It's pointless. Damn, damn, damn. . .'

He removed his hands, stripped off his gloves and stepped back, only then noticing the stricken parents still standing near the door. He lifted his hands helplessly.

'I'm sorry — we did everything we could.'

'Oh, thank God it's over,' his mother said unsteadily, and then the tears overflowed and ran down her pale cheeks.

Kathleen carefully covered the shattered body with the blanket, but left his face uncovered. Relatives hated to see a sheet over the faces of their loved ones. It was illogical, but quite understandable, and she respected that. Sticking her head out of the door, she summoned a nurse and got her to take the young man's parents back to the interview-room and give them a cup of tea.

They cleaned themselves up quickly, instructed all the others to shower again as thoroughly as possible in view of the AIDS risk, and then went into the interview room to talk to Steve's parents.

Jack was astonishing. All day long she had wondered how he had managed to bamboozle his way into a consultancy, but first the calm, unflappable way he had dealt with Steve and now here, with the devastated relatives, Kathleen had an opportunity to see at first hand the qualities that set him apart as a consultant.

He talked through the whole drama again with them, explaining the various problems their son had had, discussing the probable outcome of each of his injuries had he survived, and then, when there was no doubt left in their minds that he should have died, he gave them even more.

'Whatever problems you've had in the past, remember that he loved you, and you loved him. No one can ever take that from you.'

It was a calculated tear-jerker, but delivered with great sincerity, and Kathleen found her own eyes misting over.

She escaped to her office as soon as the Blowers' left, grabbing herself a cup of coffee on the way. Seconds later there was a tap on her door and Jack came in.

'Are you OK? You looked a bit shaken up.'

'Oh, yes, I'm fine. It all adds variety. You know what they say — the spice of life, and all that. . .'

Her voice cracked and she cleared her throat.

He gave a grim little smile. 'If you say so, Irish. Got any of that coffee left?'

She handed him the cup and he swallowed the remains with a gulp.

'Home, I think. Fancy a drink on the way?'

She remembered their inauspicious start, and her somewhat ungracious behaviour during the morning. Perhaps it would be an opportunity to smooth things over, to apologise again and make a fresh start.

Her mouth was opening, the reply ready, when there was a tap on the door.

'Ah, Mr Lawrence—there's a young man who'd like to talk to you. His name's Danny Featherstone. I think he's a friend of Steven Blowers.'

He nodded at the receptionist. 'Put him in my office. I'll be along in a tick.'

He turned back to Kathleen and shrugged.

'Sorry.'

She took a deep breath.

'Maybe later?'

He shook his head slightly. 'Some other time, perhaps. I don't know if I'd be very good company tonight after all. I'll see you.'

And with that, he was gone.

CHAPTER TWO

THERE was a strange car in the consultant's slot the following day.

Kathleen found herself heaving a sigh of relief. If he had come by car, then she wouldn't have to endure the sight of him in all that black leather gear looking like something from Star Wars. All he needed was a sweeping black cloak. . .

She hauled herself back to reality. Damn the man. He was persecuting her, and he didn't even know it! She hadn't been able to sleep at all the night before for thinking of him, and some of her thoughts had been unprintable.

But then, yesterday had been a funny old day, clouded as it was by the memory of Steve Blower's traumatic and tragic death and the image of Jack comforting his parents. It seemed inconceivable that the man who had teased her so unforgivably in the morning had been so filled with compassionate understanding later in the same day. She had had him pegged as an emotional lightweight, probably good at his job in a technical sense but untroubled by messy feelings.

Instead, he had proved himself to be capable of great human emotion. Odd, that. Jim had been good with relatives, but Jack had some extra dimension to add to it.

She had pondered on it all night — that and the image

of his laughing eyes and the way his full, firm lips tipped so readily into that wickedly sexy smile.

Just a flirt, she chastised herself, and probably a married flirt for all that. After all, he must be pushing forty at the very least to be a consultant in A and E, although he didn't look it by any stretch of the imagination.

Well, only the once, when Steven Blowers had died and he had looked up at the parents, and then a curious bleakness had stolen over his face and drained the life away. Then he had looked older.

With a sigh, she got out of the car and locked it, walking deliberately by his car to peer curiously inside.

It was a very ordinary car, a middle of the range Ford in deep blue metallic with a roof-rack on it and the back full of — ropes? How odd.

She made her way into the department, greeting all the staff with a smile and a friendly word. Amy Winship was on earlies, and flashed her a grin.

'Morning, Sister.'

'Good morning, Amy. Is Mr Lawrence in his office?'

'No, he's gone to get some breakfast. He arrived at four, apparently. There was a pile-up — they called him in.'

She nodded. Yes, he would certainly earn his keep in this job, she thought drily.

She went into her office and took the report from the night sister, then swung cheerfully into her routine.

She was busy taking off a back-slab and replastering a fracture when Jack appeared, sticking his head round the door and grinning.

'Morning, Irish.'

She shot him a black look and squeezed the water

out of a bandage viciously. 'Good morning, *sir*!' she said pointedly.

His grin widened. 'Having fun?'

'Absolutely. Want to help?'

He shook his head. 'You're managing just fine, I'd only get in your way. I'll watch, though.'

And he did, propping himself up against the wall and chatting lightheartedly to the patient while she wound the plaster bandage round the broken wrist.

'There,' she said with a smile when she had finished. 'We'll let that set for a little while, then X-ray it again to check that it's nicely lined up. OK?'

The patient, a woman in her forties, nodded. 'Thank you both. It feels much better already than it did yesterday.'

Kathleen forced a smile, showed the lady to the waiting area outside the X-ray room and went back to clear up her mess.

'Thank you both, indeed!' she muttered.

'I did talk to her to set her at her ease,' he justified mildly.

Kath snorted. 'She was already at her ease, *sir*, and while we're on the subject of putting people at their ease, my name is Sister Hennessy!'

He grinned, totally unabashed. 'I'll try and remember that, Irish.'

She wondered if she would lose her job if she tossed a sodden plaster bandage right at his grinning mouth.

Probably, but by God, it would be worth it!

A brow twitched. 'I wouldn't,' he warned softly.

She lost the battle and laughed. 'Now, would I?'

'Quite likely!'

She met his eyes, searching for any lingering trace of

the bleakness she had seen the night before, but there was none, only undiluted wickedness flirting with her senses.

Well, he was wasting his time because as far as he was concerned she had no senses left!

She wiped the sink down viciously. 'Can I do anything for you?'

He chuckled. 'Now that's a thought to play with!' he said softly.

'Damn it, Jack Lawrence ——'

She turned, the soggy, dripping plaster bandage in her hand, but he was gone, only the last swoosh of the swing door left to show he had ever been there.

She sighed and shook her head. Aggravating man. She mustn't let him take the rise out of her like that. He just seemed to find it so infuriatingly *easy*!

She caught up with him later in the staff-room, cracking jokes about second-rate coffee.

'So,' she said, 'how did you get on with that young man's friend last night?'

His face lost its sparkle. 'Ah, Danny. Well, he was very distressed, as you can imagine. They'd been lovers for some time, apparently. A few months ago they had a row, and Steve stormed off and went nightclubbing in London for the weekend. He caught HIV from a casual encounter, didn't realise and they patched up the row. The rest, as they say, is history.'

She shook her head slowly. 'How sad—what a dreadful waste.'

'One of the dangers of casual, unprotected sex. If you're going to live that life, you have to learn to do so responsibly.

'You don't have to engage in casual relationships,' she replied, more sharply than she had intended.

He arched a brow. 'Tut, tut, Sister Hennessy. Your Catholic upbringing is showing.'

'And what if it is?' she retorted, her chin lifting.

He met her eyes reprovingly. 'We're here to help, not to pass judgement. It's no business of ours to referee lifestyles.'

'But that's nonsense! I wouldn't hesitate to tell an overweight, unfit man that he was putting his health at risk. Why should I be allowed to give him dietary advice and not be able to advise a young person not to engage in indiscriminate sexual activity?'

He grinned. 'You don't tell an overweight man not to eat, you tell him what he can eat *safely*. *Ergo*, when you give advice on sexual behaviour, you don't say, "You mustn't", you say, "Do it like this"—likewise junkies. You have to give them clean needles and good habits, not moral outrage and prohibition.'

'Who in the hell is talking about moral outrage?' she demanded, her voice rising.

He just grinned wider, bent forwards and dropped a kiss on her startled lips.

'Beautiful,' he murmured absently, and walked away, leaving her riveted to the spot, astonished.

'Well, well, well—I do believe our dear Sister Hennessy is speechless!'

She glared at Ben Bradshaw, dragged some air into her deprived lungs and marched swiftly down the corridor into her office, shutting the door firmly behind her.

Then she let out the breath and sagged against the desk. Dazed, she lifted her fingers and rested them against her lips. They felt—tinglingly alive, soft and warm and swollen, aching for—for what? For more?

With a whimper of disgust and confusion, she sank into her chair and stared absently at the mound of paperwork. Damn him. Why did he have to do that? As if he'd known she'd spent all night wondering about the feel of his lips on hers, about how it would be if he kissed her.

She'd never expected rockets to go off and stars to shoot in all directions—leastways, not from just a casual brush of flesh against flesh. . .

She suppressed a shiver. Damn him. There had been nothing casual about that kiss. Brief, yes, and out-wardly innocent, but my God, packed with promise!

Well, it wasn't about to happen again!

She got to her feet, checked her cap in the little mirror on the wall and marched out into her department.

She rapped on his door, swung it open and stood in the doorway, not trusting either of them if it was shut.

He raised his eyes from the paperwork on his desk and leant back in the chair, a lazy grin on his face.

'I suppose you want an apology?' he said unrepentantly.

'Don't you ever—ever!—pull a stunt like that again!'

The grin widened. 'Sorry—didn't you enjoy it? Per-haps next time——'

'Didn't you hear me?' she returned, her voice torn between a growl and a whimper. 'There will be no next time!'

'Pity. I was rather looking forward to it.'

She glared at him. 'You're incorrigible.'

He shrugged, a laughing, arrogant, almost Gallic

shrug. You would have thought it was a compliment, she thought crossly.

'I try to be.'

'Well, don't. This is my department, and I won't have you lolling around here undermining my authority—'

'My dear girl, nothing I could do could possibly undermine your authority,' he drawled lazily. 'The entire department cowers at the sound of your voice. I should have thought a little evidence of human frailty would merely enhance your reputation—and the association would do mine a power of good!'

She snorted. 'Your reputation would be greatly enhanced if you took yourself seriously!'

Something changed in his face then, some fleeting spectre that drained the life from his eyes and left them cold and hard.

Then he smiled, a dangerous, cynical smile.

'Life's too short to take it seriously, Irish. You should learn that, before it's too late.'

And with that he picked up his pen and returned to his paperwork, dismissing her.

She was in the staff lounge making herself a drink when he came in half an hour later.

'Coffee?' she asked, more as a reflex than anything. He shuddered and shook his head.

'Think I'll pass. Actually, I wanted to talk to you about yesterday. What's hospital policy on HIV testing after an incident like yesterday?'

'I don't think we have a policy. It's never been a problem before. If someone knows they've been contaminated by a needle or a knife, for instance, then I think the testing certainly is available.'

'But not otherwise?'

She shook her head. 'No. Why should it be necessary? I mean, I don't think anyone took any risks, and we were all wearing gloves anyway because of the state he was in — I would be worried that it would make people panic unnecessarily. You know, rather like getting an adverse smear test, and before you know where you are you've convinced yourself you've got cancer when it was probably just a lousy smear and they didn't get enough cells. Do you understand what I'm saying? I don't think we should threaten people's conception of their immortality unnecessarily, and I'm perfectly certain we're all quite safe.'

He shrugged. 'It was just an idea. Professionally, if I felt there was a risk I should want to know that I was clear so I was certain there was no danger of me passing anything on to a patient or a future partner. I mean, if you did contract it, wouldn't you want to know?'

She met his eye determinedly. 'Of course, if I felt there was a real risk, but I wouldn't pass it on anyway. I'm extremely careful at work and I don't have indiscriminate sexual relationships.'

He laughed softly, and it tickled up her spine. 'Your rosary's showing again, Irish. I didn't say anything about *indiscriminate* sex. Take Ben, for example. He's married. I gather his wife's pregnant. Now how would he feel if he contracted the virus from a freak accident at work and gave it to his wife and child just because we had failed to test him?'

Kath stared at him, stupefied. 'Maggie's pregnant? When?'

He grinned lazily. 'Well, I hardly liked to ask him *that*!'

She clicked her tongue irritably. 'You know what I mean. . .'

'Ask him—I'm sure it's not a secret.'

'I wonder why he hasn't said anything?' Kath mused.

'I think they only knew this morning, and you've been so busy being cross——'

'Huh! How would you like it if you were sexually harrassed?'

He grinned again. 'Try me.'

She drew herself up and sniffed. 'Don't be absurd. Why would I want to do that?'

'Because you're curious? Because you're secretly dying to press that delightful body up against me and find out how it feels?'

He was so close to the truth that she flushed and looked away. 'Please,' she muttered in a strangled voice. 'You're embarrassing me.'

His deep chuckle curled round her insides and squeezed. 'I'm sorry. I'll leave you in peace with your atrocious coffee.'

Her head came up. 'Jack?'

He stopped and looked back over his shoulder. 'Hmm?'

'About the testing—do you really think it's necessary?'

'In this case, no, but I think we should keep an open mind if anyone asks. I doubt if they will, but just keep your ears open.'

She nodded, and with a wink, he was gone, leaving

her dealing with her curiosity about how his body *would* feel pressed against hers, and the slow recognition that the coffee was, indeed, atrocious.

'Who is he, do we know?'

The ambulanceman shook his head. 'Collapsed in the park. Nobody knows him, no ID. Passer-by saw him and reported him—thought he was drunk. He was unconscious when we got to him.'

'Right, thank you, Sid.'

Kathleen bent over the unconscious patient and sniffed. No alcohol, but he was clammy and grey, and quite likely hypoglaecaemic. There was a pin-prick hole in the tip of his left thumb, and she nodded. Diabetic, gone into a coma from low blood sugar. She left the cubicle to find a blood test kit, and came back to find the new houseman, Joe Reynolds, ordering head X-rays and a neurologist's opinion.

She rolled her eyes and wondered how to tackle it. Young doctors were usually only too willing to take advice, but every now and again you got one like this lad, who clearly was all at sea and didn't know how to light the flares!

'Not a bad idea,' she said, 'considering he's probably banged his head when he passed out. Diabetics often damage themselves, don't they?'

He looked faintly startled. 'Diabetics? Does he have a Medic Alert bracelet?'

'I have no idea, but he——'

'Well, then, I think it would be safer to assume a neurological cause such as CVA, don't you, Sister?' he said loftily.

'Certainly, *Doctor*, if you say so,' she replied

sweetly, containing the urge to crown him for his patronising ignorance. After all, how long would it take to do a blood test with a Haemastix strip? Thirty seconds? What he was planning would tie half the hospital up for the entire morning!

Jack was busy, dealing with a nasty fracture, so she went to the nursing station and picked up the phone. 'Page Dr Marumba for me, could you?' she asked the switchboard. Seconds later she was connected to the consultant physician.

'Are you busy, Jesus? I wonder if I could offer you a cup of coffee in my department within the next couple of minutes?'

There was a deep chuckle from the other end. 'My pleasure, Kathleen. Problems?'

'You might say that.'

'Be right down.'

'Bless you.'

She put the receiver down and went back into the cubicle. 'Should we take some bloods for chemistry, Dr Reynolds?' she asked mildly.

'Ah — good idea, Sister. Perhaps you'd like to do the honours?'

'Certainly.' She withdrew fifty millilitres of completely unnecessary blood from the patient's arm, filled up the appropriate bottles and then put a blob on the treated strip and glanced at her watch.

As she finished she heard Dr Marumba's deep, cultured rumble in the corridor.

She stuck her head round the curtain and winked. 'Nearly done here, Dr Marumba. Could you give me a minute?'

'Sure.' The tall man elbowed his way past the curtain

and peered at the patient. 'Interesting — looks like hypoglycaemia, doesn't it, Dr Reynolds?'

The SHO's jaw dropped. 'Ah — um — well, it's certainly a possibility, sir.'

Jesus nodded. 'Oh, yes, see the strip — blood sugar way down. Well spotted. I see Sister Hennessy's done all the necessary tests for you. Well done. Glucagon?'

'Ah — well, yes, I ——'

'Good, good. Well, I mustn't hold you up. Perhaps I'll come by for coffee another time, Sister. I can see you're busy here with Dr Reynolds.' He brushed past Kathleen, and the orthodontic miracle of his smile flashed against the rich ebony of his skin. His wink was wickedly conspiratorial.

'I'm sorry about the coffee,' she apologised, working hard on her straight face.

'Forget it — it's better upstairs, anyway.'

'Not you, too!' She turned back to Joe Reynolds and smiled innocently.

He returned the smile warily. 'I guess I owe you an apology, Sister.'

She let her smile mellow. Poor boy, he had no idea his downfall had been engineered. 'Think nothing of it,' she told him. 'I've been doing the job for years, don't forget. Experience counts for a lot, Joe. OK, what next?'

He opened his mouth, shut it again and grinned sheepishly.

'Glucagon?'

She waited.

'Um. . .'

'We'll go through it together, shall we? Then he can go and rest in the day ward for a while.'

The relief on Joe's face would have been comic if it hadn't been so worrying. Yet another one she was going to have to watch like a hawk, she thought wearily. Between him and Amy Winship, they were well staffed with idiots at the moment.

Oh, well, it would give her two bodyguards if she didn't ever let them out of her sight. That way she might have some protection against Jack Lawrence and his hyperactive lips!

It worked till Thursday, but then Amy was on days off and Joe had a cold. Inevitably it meant that she and Jack were in closer proximity, and it threatened to push her sanity over the brink.

Though why it should, lord only knows, she thought. What is it the man has that's so darned appealing?

Charm, her alter ego told her. Lazy, sexy, masculine charm — bucketfuls of it, coupled with a certain vulnerability that showed every now and then. Unfortunately it was a potent combination, and there was no known cure.

By about two-thirty she had run out of ways of dodging him. They had a patient with multiple lacerations of the face and neck following a fall through a window, and he needed extensive suturing. Never having seen Jack suture, she wondered if she ought to call the fascio-maxillary surgeon over from the Norfolk and Norwich, or if she could, indeed, trust Jack to do a decent job. Their own fascio-max man was on holiday that week or the problem wouldn't have arisen.

She decided there was only one way to deal with it, and that was directly.

She found him in his office.

'How's your suturing?' she asked without preamble.

'My suturing? Pretty good — why?'

'We have a patient with multiple lacerations of the face and neck and our fascio-max is away — I was just wondering if you were good enough,' she replied bluntly.

He smiled — which was just as well. He could have flipped, having his professional competence challenged like that.

'I think she'll be safe with mc,' hc said mildly.

'He.'

'Even better. I'll practise on the jaw-line — then if it isn't good enough, he can always grow a beard to hide it.'

His voice was so bland she really wasn't sure if he was joking, but having asked and received an apparently satisfactory reply, she decided she had no choice but to go with him.

'He's in Cubicle Four.'

Jack nodded. 'I'll have a look, but then I think we'll move him into Ops if I think it's justified. I'll need a good work light.'

He went in to the patient, a man in his thirties, and smiled a hello.

'I was enjoying that cup of tea,' he said mournfully.

The man attempted a smile. 'Sorry, Guv. Made a bit of a mess, haven't I?'

'Just a shade. Still, soon have you sorted out. I think we'll move you into a little theatre we have down here for just this sort of thing, OK? I'll get the nurses to move you and get you comfy, and I'll have a bit of a wash and change. See you in a tick.'

By the time Kathleen had sorted the patient out and

found someone to give his wife a cup of tea and explain what was happening, Jack was back in Theatre, clad from head to toe in green theatre pyjamas, with a J-cloth hat and a mask.

'Good, ennit? Just like the telly,' he said to the man, and received a lopsided grin for his pains. 'You know, you really ought to do something about that razor you've been using!'

The man chuckled. Kath knew what Jack was doing, unobtrusively trying to assess the range of movement and any possible nerve damage indicated by loss of mobility in any of the facial muscles.

She relaxed. Already gowned and masked herself, she drew up the lignocaine and opened the suture packs.

Three hours later Jack tied the last suture and stood back to survey his work.

'Bee-ootiful.'

It was. Oh, the patient looked a mess, but Kath had seen the enormous care that had gone into the alignment of each suture, the meticulous attention not only to the innumerable tiny little muscle fibres, nerves and blood vessels but to laughter lines and wrinkles to ensure that the tissues were realigned as closely as possible to their original position. He sealed the whole area with plastic skin to prevent infection, and then stripped off his gloves and stretched.

'Thank you, Doctor,' the patient said a little stiffly. He was going to find it rather difficult to talk for a few days, Kathleen realised.

Jack smiled warmly. 'My pleasure. I'm afraid you won't be Miss World again, but you'll do. All adds character. Come back in a week for a check-up and to have the majority of the sutures out, or earlier if they give you any trouble or get infected. Try and keep them dry, and take the painkillers we'll give you for the first few days. How did you get here?'

'My wife drove me.'

He nodded. 'Good. Well, get her to take you home and look after you. You'll be off work for a week. Sister will give you a certificate, and you'll need a follow-up next time you come if you're still a bit sore. Hopefully you won't need it.'

With a cheery wave he left them, and Kathleen helped the man to his feet and put him in a wheelchair.

'Don't want you collapsing on us — not good for the department's reputation,' she joked lightly, and wheeled him round and handed him over to his wife.

She found Jack in his office, leaning on the window with a cigarette in his hand.

'You smoke!' she said in horror.

'Only under duress. That was a long old job. Thanks for your help.'

'You're welcome. You did it well. I'm sorry I asked you if you were good enough.'

He chuckled. 'Your privilege, my darling girl. I hope you aren't going to find me anything else to do tonight.'

'Why, tired?'

He grinned. 'No, I was hoping you'd join me for that drink.'

She was caught without defences, her mind still playing with the idea of being his darling girl.

'Ah — drink?' she said helplessly.

'Yes, you know, as in go into a pub and order something in a glass and eat a few nuts and so on.'

She wasn't sure about the 'and so on', but there

didn't seem to be any way out of it without being churlish.

'Um—perhaps just a quick one. . .'

'Am I treading on anyone's toes?'

'Toes?'

'Yes, toes. As in, some resident lover or whatever— perhaps Mick O'Shea?'

'Mick?' She was startled.

He shrugged. 'You were all over each other on Monday morning.'

'Oh, that—no, Mick's a friend.'

His brow arched delicately.

'Truly! I've known him for years.' She eyed Jack suspiciously. 'What about you? I don't suppose you're married?' she said bluntly.

He threw back his head and laughed. 'Are you crazy? Why would I want a wife?'

She shrugged. 'I don't know. Why would anybody want a wife? I'm sure there are all manner of reasons.'

He chuckled. 'None good enough for me, I'm afraid. Never again.'

'So you're divorced?'

He nodded.

'I'm not going to bed with you.'

He blinked, and caught the smile before it got away. 'Of course not.'

'I mean it!'

He grinned wickedly. 'What d'you think I'm going to do, drag you behind a hanging basket and rip your knickers off?'

The image was so outrageous that she giggled. 'All right. What time?'

'Seven-thirty? Do you want me to pick you up?'

'On that bike? No way, *José*. Just tell me where.'

'Rose and Crown, Tuddingfield?'

She nodded. 'OK. I'll see you there at seven-thirty.'

Deciding she was crazy, she made her way back to her room, collected her things and was just about to leave when a man carrying a young boy walked up to the doors.

He looked a little lost, and Kathleen went up to him.

'Can I help you, sir?'

'Oh — it's my son — he's got cystic fibrosis, and my wife's gone away for a few days with a friend for a break. I thought I could cope, but they sent him home from school and I just can't seem to shift the stuff off his lungs.'

Indeed, the child was rattling and bubbling, coughing weakly and obviously in great discomfort.

Kathleen put her arm round the man's shoulders and led him in.

'Come round here with me, and we'll find a physio to take care of things for you. What's his name? Do we have any notes on him in the hospital?'

'Anthony Craven — yes, you've got stacks of notes. I'm sorry, I feel such a fool. I was sure I could cope but the CF clinic people had all gone home by the time I realised I couldn't manage——'

'Look, don't worry, it really isn't a problem. I'll get a physio. You sit in here with Anthony and I'll be back in a tick.'

She put him in the cubicle and went back to the nursing station to phone the physiotherapy department.

After a few seconds she glanced at her watch in disgust. It was just after six, long after the time she should have gone off duty, and that was exactly what all the physiotherapists had done. She would have handed over to one of her colleagues, but somehow she just felt this case needed her personal attention.

She called the switchboard and asked them to page the physio on call, and was told she was in ITU with a patient and likely to be tied up for at least half an hour.

She cradled the phone with more force than strictly necessary, just as Jack Lawrence strolled past in his black leather gear.

'Problems?' he asked.

She glanced up. Nothing compared to what her heart did when she looked at him like that. He was long overdue for a shave, and the combination of the dark stubble, the tousled hair from the theatre cap and the warm smell of leather was a potent combination.

She shook her head. 'Not really. I want a physio for a kid with cystic fibrosis, but she's down in ITU and won't be free for half an hour.'

Something happened in his eyes then, some kind of inner battle. It was evidently resolved, because a sort of gentle resignation settled over his features.

'Where is he? I'll do it.'

'In Three, but are you sure you know——?'

He laughed, a short, strained little laugh. 'You really don't have any faith at all in me, do you?' he said, and his voice sounded strangely sad. 'Trust me. It isn't something you easily forget,' he added enigmatically, and with that he turned on his heel and strode back down to his office, emerging a moment later back in his normal working clothes.

The harassed father was only too glad to hand over as Jack tenderly lifted the boy, laid him on his side over some foam blocks and firmly but gently percussed his chest.

Kath watched, mesmerised. He seemed to know just where to tap, and how hard, and how long for, and bit by bit the boy's lungs cleared and he began to breathe more easily.

When he was finished he sat the boy up and tousled his hair. 'OK, son? Come back in the morning and we'll sort you out again.'

And with that he was gone, back to his office to re-don his leathers.

Kathleen emerged from the cloakroom with her things just as he was walking past, and she went with him out of the door. He didn't break his stride or slow down, and she practically had to run to keep up with him, but something in the set of his jaw worried her.

He stopped by the bike, taking his helmet out of one of the panniers on the back, and then swung his leg over the seat, straddling the machine easily.

'Are you OK?' she asked finally, when it was obvious he wasn't going to acknowledge her presence.

He looked up. 'Of course. Why shouldn't I be?'

His eyes had a distant, cold remoteness she hadn't seen in them before, and she knew instinctively that something was very wrong.

Before she could say any more, he settled the helmet down over his head and fastened the strap. Then rocking the bike off the centrestand, he walked it back out of the space and starting it with a throaty roar, he left her standing there.

It was sheer, blind gut instinct that made her go to the porter's lodge and lie.

'Could you give me Mr Lawrence's address? He's

left something here and I know he'll want it — I thought
I'd drop it in to him. I have to go out that way tonight.'

He flicked open a card index, scribbled an address
and phone number and handed it to her.

'Thanks, that's great.'

The old porter grinned and winked and opened his
mouth. Kath ran before he had time to air his sugges-
tive remark.

She was at the pub in the village at seven-thirty, but
she was pretty sure he wouldn't show. There was no
sign of either his car or the bike, and she waited until
eight-fifteen.

Then, her heart in her mouth, she went into the pub,
located the public call box in the lobby and dialled the
number the porter had given her.

It was picked up on the fourth ring by an answerphone. She listened to his voice, waited for the tone
and then cradled the receiver gently.

She knew he was there. Something — that same gut
instinct that made her get his address alerted her. She
looked at the address. Lone Barn, Finningham Lane,
Tuddingfield. Well, she was in Tuddingfield, and she'd
seen the turning off to Finningham. All she needed
now was Lone Barn.

Thoughtfully, she went back out to her car, got
behind the wheel and drove slowly out of the village,
turning down the narrow, winding lane to Finningham.

She saw it almost immediately, the black wooden
structure in sharp relief against the evening sky. Lone
Barn indeed. It was set in the middle of a corn field,
and she turned between the tall stalks of corn and
followed the track up to the barn.

There were no lights on, but the bike and car were

there, parked in an open-sided barn, and the door to the house was hanging open.

She wiped her damp palms against the skirt of her dress and drew a deep breath, then got out.

'Here goes,' she muttered to herself, and walked slowly up to the door.

CHAPTER THREE

HE KNEW she was there long before he saw her. He had been dimly aware of the sound of an approaching car, and there was only one person who would have bothered to seek him out. She would have had to charm his address out of the porter, but she wouldn't have had any trouble doing that. Lord, no.

He lifted his head.

Dear God, she was lovely. Sweetly pretty, in her full flowered dress that hung in soft folds around her slender legs. The slanting sun was behind her, and as she stood there in the doorway he could see the outline of those smooth, slim thighs through the fine fabric. His gut clenched, and he forced his eyes up to her face. Her eyes were huge, almost luminous in the shadowy light.

He drew a deep breath and reached for the tumbler of Scotch beside him.

'You didn't turn up,' she said in her soft, lilting voice.

'You didn't expect me to.'

'No.' She crossed the room and sat opposite him in the ratty old armchair. 'Nice place.'

He glanced around, conscious only of her. 'Mmm.'

'I like the brick floor, and all the wood. It suits you.'

'Earthy and unfinished. It'll be better when I've finished unpacking.'

Their eyes met, and his slid away. Damn, he wanted
her.

'Are you very drunk?'

'I'm working on it.'

'It won't help, you know.'

He took a hefty swallow and crashed the glass back
down. 'You're out of order, Irish.'

'I don't think so. I think something's eating you, and
I think you ought to talk about it.'

'I don't want to talk about it. I want to sit here and
get stinking drunk and forget.'

He lifted the glass again but it was empty. He lit a
cigarette instead.

He could hear her sharply indrawn breath, the effort
it took not to comment. Good, he thought, if I really
work on her she'll go away and leave me to it.

'Do you know what I really want? You — your body,
hot and naked and writhing under me — '

'You won't drive me out, Jack. Anyway, I'm quite
safe. You haven't got any hanging baskets.'

He chuckled despite himself. God, she had guts. Or
perhaps she just didn't realise how close to the edge he
really was. . .

'Damn it, Irish, go home,' he said wearily.

'No. Let me make you some coffee.'

'I don't want coffee, I want to be alone — savvy? By
myself. I don't want you here. Please leave.'

She was in the kitchen area now, divided from the
rest of the downstairs by a row of cupboards that ran
out at waist-height halfway across the room. She eyed
him over the top.

'Where do you keep the coffee?'

'You don't give up, do you?' he said bitterly.

'Not easily,' she said blithely. 'All those years of training.'

She found the coffee without his help and put the kettle on.

He ground out the cigarette and watched her, the burning need in him too fierce to ignore. She had switched on the light and as she walked back towards him, he could see her legs again through the dress. Her soft fragrance drifted towards him, light and yet intoxicating, summer flowers and sun-warmed skin. God, he wanted her.

'Here.'

She held out the coffee but he didn't take it, not daring to trust himself if he reached towards her.

He closed his eyes wearily, but his eyelids acted only as shutters for his eyes, not his mind. He could still see her quite clearly, the outline of her legs, the soft rise and fall of her breasts with her gentle breathing, the way she looked at him, like a rabbit with a rattlesnake, half afraid and yet too fascinated to run.

He heard the coffee-cup as she put it down, then the soft swish of her skirt as she crossed the room and sat on the chair again. The light movement of air drifted her scent across his face, and he sucked the air in greedily.

'Talk to me.'

'No. Go home.'

'I don't think you really want me to.'

His eyes opened and he glowered at her, despairing. 'You don't know what I want.'

'Need, then. Whatever it is, you need to talk to someone. I'm here.'

'I'd noticed,' he growled, and dropped his head back

against the cushion. Why wouldn't she go home? She'd slipped her shoes off and had her feet tucked under her bottom, her legs demurely covered by that gauzy dress, but it was too late, he'd seen. . .

'Drink your coffee.'

'Damn it, I don't *want* any coffee!' he snarled, and she blinked.

'OK, don't drink it. I don't care.'

Their eyes met, hers wary, his angry and resentful, defensive. He felt trapped, cornered.

She wriggled in the chair and he caught a flash of silken thigh before she settled again. His body roared to life, hard and urgent, over-riding the pain. He shifted awkwardly, and her eyes flew to his lap and then up to his face, wide and slightly startled, like a doe.

'What's the matter, Irish? It's only basic human biology—nothing you haven't seen before.'

She looked away, flushing. 'Don't be coarse. I only wanted to help you.'

He was instantly ashamed. 'Look, I'm sorry,' he said heavily, 'but I don't need your help. What I need is to be alone.'

'So you can drink yourself into a stupor?'

'Yes, damn it, if that's what it takes!'

'To do what?'

He glared at her. 'Leave it, Kath,' he warned.

'No,' she said softly. 'Jack, I can't. . .'

She was breathing fast, her breasts rising and falling against the soft cotton, and suddenly he couldn't breathe, couldn't sit there another moment and watch her. . .

'For Christ's sake, get out,' he muttered, and levering himself out of the chair, he crossed the room in a stride and climbed the open stairs three at a time.

It was a mistake. He should have gone outside, grabbed the keys of the bike and taken off, but instead he was trapped and she was following him, her footsteps tentative on the stairs.

'Jack? Let me help you. . .'

She was either very stupid or very brave. He couldn't decide which. Pain and need were rising up in equal measure to swamp him, and he knew he didn't have what it took to turn away from her.

He threw himself down on the huge old bed and stared at the sloping timber ceiling. Oh, God, get her out of here, he prayed, but she kept on coming.

He felt the bed dip slightly under her weight, and he knew she was kneeling beside him. Her touch on his shoulder was hesitant, light as a butterfly, but it was enough.

With a deep groan he reached up and pulled her down beside him.

'Damn you, Irish,' he whispered hoarsely, and then his lips found hers and everything else receded.

Oh, God, she was so soft and supple, her body arching against his, trembling like a reed in the wind. She met his kiss eagerly, her hands tangled in his hair, and the last remnant of resistance snapped.

His hand slid up her thigh and found fine silk and lace in his way. And buttons. He despatched them and groaned again. So soft, so warm, so irresistible. He could lose himself in that sweetness, maybe even forget, for a while. . .

He wrenched his jeans down and moved over her, inhaling deeply. God, she smelt so sweet! Her hands were on his shoulders and she was pleading, but the words were a blur in the swirling mist of need and pain that engulfed him.

As he entered her he heard her cry out, and the sound inflamed him further, her soft whimpers slashing at the edges of his control.

So sweet, so tight — her slim, supple body writhed beneath him and he felt his control shatter into a million pieces. With a savage cry he drove into her one last time and felt the shockwaves pulse through him, draining all sensation and leaving a blessed numbness in which there was no more pain. . .

His chest heaving, he collapsed against her, the breath driven from his body, his heart thrashing against his ribs, and then slowly awareness returned, seeping into his dazed mind like ice-water, bring with it the pain and an overwhelming sense of self-loathing and disgust.

Dear God, what had he done to her?

He jerked his body away from hers and stood, dragging his jeans back up with hands that shook like leaves in a hurricane.

'Damn you,' he grated, and felt disgust like bile rising in his throat. 'Now are you satisfied?'

He heard a ragged sob, and then the bed creaked as she stood up.

'Jack. . .?'

'For Christ's sake, *get out*!' he roared, and after an interminable second, he heard her footsteps running down the stairs and then the sound of her car on the drive.

In the silence that followed he heard an owl hoot,

and then nothing, nothing except the harsh sound of someone sobbing.

'*Johnnie*!' he shouted, and the sound echoed in the stillness, bouncing off the walls and coming back to torment him.

Kathleen remembered nothing of the drive home, turning automatically into the parking area behind her flat and letting herself in with hands that shook so badly she could scarcely hold the keys.

She stripped off her clothes and dropped them where they fell, then ran a bath and climbed into it, scouring her skin over and over with a loofah as if she could wash away the memory of his body on hers.

Still trembling, she got out finally and wrapped herself in a huge towel and padded into the kitchen to put the kettle on.

God, what a fool! She should have seen it coming, should have realised she was pushing him too hard. She felt raw—not physically, except where she had scoured her skin in the bath, but inside, in her soul, as if he had reached in and desecrated some sacred part of her.

Rape.

It was a terrifying word, and yet he hadn't really raped her. Under different circumstances, even tonight, she would have been willing. . .

She laughed harshly. Willing? She had been aching for him since she had first seen him straddling that bike with such lazy arrogance. And yet, tonight, some demon that she didn't understand had driven him to an act she was sure he was now bitterly regretting.

Why had she left? She should have stayed with him,

told him she wanted to understand, held him in her arms while he released the terrible pain she had sensed inside him.

It had been in his eyes when he lay on the bed staring rigidly at the ceiling, a terrifying, heart-rending pain that cut her to the bone. And afterwards, for a second she had felt him relax against her, his body spent, his feelings so near the surface she could almost reach out and touch them, and then he had wrenched himself away from her and the defences had gone slamming back up, shutting her out.

That was what hurt.

She absently brushed the tears from her cheeks and sniffed. After all that, still he had shut her out.

'Damn you, Jack Lawrence,' she whispered. 'I won't *be* shut out!'

She dialled his number with shaking fingers and got the answerphone. 'Jack, please, pick up the phone. I know you're there. I need to talk to you. Please pick it up. I'm waiting. Jack, for God's sake —— ' Her voice cracked and she took a steadying breath. 'Jack, ring me, please!' She gave him the number, then put the phone down, crawled into bed and waited.

'Morning, Sister!'

She smiled vaguely at the porter. 'Morning, Alvin.'

'Lovely day for it,' he continued cheerfully.

'Mmm.' For what? she thought bleakly. She took the report, told them all where to find her if necessary and shut herself in her office.

The bike was outside. He was here, somewhere in the building, and sooner or later she had to face him.

Just now, assailed by a sudden attack of nerves, she hoped it would be later.

She misjudged him. There was a sharp tap on her door and it swung in, shutting quickly behind him.

She looked up and made herself meet his eyes. What she saw there left her cold.

He didn't beat about the bush.

'Kathleen, I'm sorry. I really don't know what else to say.'

She was silent for a long while, searching his face for a way forward, but it was shuttered and empty, all emotion banished. Was this the same man who had lost all control with her last night? No, not all control. He had released the pressure of his emotions in the only way a society built on a stiff upper lip had left him — but his control over his real feelings had remained even then. But what had caused that violent upsurge of emotion?

'I don't think I really want an apology, Jack,' she said calmly. 'I think what I really want is to know why.'

'How about because I'm a selfish, thoughtless, egotistical bastard, without any human decency?'

She shook her head. 'No, sorry, it won't wash.'

He laughed without humour. 'Damn it, you won't give up on me, will you?'

She sensed the frustration behind his remark, and backed off a little.

'I meant to help,' she said softly. 'If anything, I owe you an apology. I pushed you too hard. I'm sorry. . .' She reached out and laid her hand on his arm, and beneath her fingers she felt the corded muscle clench.

'How can you touch me?' he whispered harshly. 'Damn it, Kathleen, I raped you.'

'No, you didn't. Not really. I think I knew what was going to happen when I followed you upstairs. It was as much my fault as yours—probably more. At least I was sober!' She lifted her hand towards his face, and then dropped it. 'How's the head?'

He smiled ruefully. 'Lousy, thanks. I didn't have any more after you went.' He sighed. 'I owe you an explanation, don't I?'

Their eyes met and held, and gradually she saw warmth and respect creep into the granite depths.

'Tonight—can you come to the house? About seven? I'll cook you a meal.'

She hesitated, her heart pounding. What would happen, all alone with him in that isolated barn? Whatever had troubled him yesterday was still far from unresolved. Was she insane?

'You're quite safe.'

'You said that last night.'

He made a disgusted noise in the back of his throat and looked away from her.

'I know it's hard to expect you to believe it after what happened, but you can trust me. There are things at the house—things I'd like to show you.'

'Etchings?'

His mouth lifted in a token smile. 'Photos, mainly. Some drawings. Other bits and pieces.'

'OK.'

His eyes flicked back to hers, wide with disbelief. 'You will?'

She nodded. 'Is that a mistake?'

'No,' he promised fervently, and this time she believed him.

He walked back to the door. 'I have to go, Anthony

Craven's back for his physio. I said I'd do it, and I want to get some sputum samples for analysis to make sure he hasn't got a chest infection. And talking of infections, in case you're worried, you won't get anything from me — including pregnant.'

She stared at the door. Another page in the manuscript that was Jack Lawrence. She knew for a fact that he hadn't used a condom, so that meant he couldn't get her pregnant. Was that the trouble? Had Anthony Craven reminded him that he couldn't have children? Surely not. He had attended other children during the week, and been fine. And yet he had just said — she shook her head and stood up. Tonight. She only had to wait till tonight, and she would get her answers. But it was going to be a long day. . .

Not only long, but busy, filled with drama and tragedy, so that her own problems faded into insignificance.

She had been on the run since her conversation with Jack, a steady stream of nasty fractures and frightened children and anxious parents, and then, shortly after two, just when things began to settle down and she thought she might actually get some lunch, a car screeched up into the entrance and a man jumped out, flung open the back of the car and half dragged, half carried a woman towards the doors.

Kathleen called for help and ran to meet him.

'What's the matter?'

'She collapsed — said she had a pain, climbed off the ladder and passed out. We were decorating. Oh, God, is she all right?'

The porter arrived with a trolley and they lowered the woman on to it and rushed her into Resuscitation.

'Amy, get Mr Lawrence,' Kath instructed as they passed the bemused girl in the corridor.

'Yes, Sister.'

Kath heard her feet hurrying away, and snatched up the stethoscope. The woman's heart was still beating, but erratically.

'Is she on any drugs?'

He shook his head.

'Contraceptive pill?'

'No — I've had a vasectomy.'

'How old is she?'

'Thirty-seven — nearly thirty-eight.'

'And you're her husband?'

'Yes, that's right. My name's Thompson — Brian Thompson. My wife's Angie.'

Amy reappeared. 'Mr Lawrence is just coming.'

'Good. Thank you. Amy, take Mr Thompson and get all his wife's details from him, please, and then see if you can find any notes. Reception will help you.'

Jack arrived as Amy and Mr Thompson left.

'What is it?'

'Chest pain, sudden onset as far as I know, collapse — she's now arrhythmic, possibly fibrillating.'

All the while she was talking Kathleen was undressing the woman. Once she had stripped off her top clothes she slapped the monitor pads on and connected up the leads.

Jack whistled softly. 'What a mess! She's definitely fibrillating — I'd say she's had an MI.'

Kath nodded. 'Looks like it, doesn't it?'

'We'll give her a belt, see if that stops it.' He twiddled the dials on the defibrillator and told Kath to stand back. As he touched the paddles to the woman's chest wall, her body arched and flopped, and the trace immediately altered, settling to a normal sinus rhythm.

'So far so good. Can you take some bloods for chemistry, and we'll start her on streptokinase. Maybe that'll hold her. Who's on take today?'

'Jesus Marumba. I'll call him down.'

She moved to the phone on the wall and called the switchboard, asking them to page the physician, and then turned back to their patient.

She looked really grim — cold, clammy, grey. . .

She met Jack's eyes, and he shook his head. 'I wonder if she has any history?'

'Her husband didn't mention it, and you'd think he would.'

Amy slipped back in then. 'Records are sending her notes up now. Seems she's been seeing Mr Marumba for a few months. Her husband didn't know.'

Jack and Kathleen exchanged glances.

'What did you tell him?

She looked instantly alarmed. 'Nothing — I asked if he knew if she'd seen anyone in the hospital recently, before we contacted Records. He said no. I haven't spoken to him since — oh, except to say I'd find out what I could.'

Kath relaxed. 'OK, Amy. Well, she's still not really conscious, but he could come in for a minute, couldn't he?' Her eyes met Jack's, and he nodded.

'I'll get him,' Amy said, and vanished.

There was a sudden, yawning silence broken only by the slight hiss of oxygen to the mask over Mrs Thompson's face.

Their eyes were still meshed and Kath found she was unable to look away. The earlier remoteness was gone, replaced instead by a naked vulnerability that shook her.

'Did I hurt you?' he asked gruffly.

She looked away then, shaken by the memory of his body tangling so intimately with her. 'No,' she whispered. 'No, you didn't hurt me.'

She glanced at the monitor. 'That really isn't a very healthy wave,' she said in a slightly firmer voice.

After a second he shifted his eyes. 'No. We'll see what Marumba says.'

But he didn't get there in time. Seconds after Mr Thompson came back in with Amy, Mrs Thompson suffered a second, massive heart attack. Kath snapped instructions to everyone, and Amy wheeled Mr Thompson out and took him to the interview-room.

Despite desperate attempts to revive her, the trace remained stubbornly flat, until in the end they had to give up. Kath looked up at Jack in despair.

'She's thirty-seven. That's so bloody unfair!'

He sighed shortly. 'Life is. At least it was quick.'

'That's better than knowing, than having time to prepare?'

'You can never prepare. You think you can, but you can't. It's the finality of it. That's what gets you, no matter how much warning you might think you've had.'

He walked away, thrusting the swing door out of his way and striding off down the corridor towards his office.

Amy coughed. 'Um — her husband's in the interview-room, Sister.'

Kath looked at her blankly. 'What? Oh, right. Thank you, Amy. Could you stay here for a minute? I'll go and talk to him.'

She followed Jack out, glancing down the corridor after him. What had he meant? Because there was no doubt in her mind that he had been talking from personal experience.

Was that the problem? She glanced at her watch. Only three more hours to go, and she would find out.

She wore jeans and a sweatshirt that night — and then felt foolish because she knew he would realise instantly why she was covering herself from head to toe. She just felt it would help to establish some boundaries, and just then she felt they both needed space to get over the incident.

It hadn't stopped her putting on make-up, though, just a touch of eyeshadow and mascara, and a tiny puff of perfume at the base of her throat.

He was outside turning food on a barbecue when she drove up, and he lifted his hand and walked over to her.

She was glad they were outside, away from the scene of the crime, so to speak. She got out of the car and he stooped and brush his lips against her cheek. A little tingle teased her skin, and she was burningly conscious of the touch of his hand on her arm.

'Thank you for coming — I wasn't sure you would.'

'I said I would,' she reminded him, and he smiled wryly.

'I should have known better than to think you'd back down.'

She chuckled. 'That's me, in there to the bitter end, like a terrier. The only trouble is, I don't know when to stop.'

His thumb caressed her arm absently as he looked

down at her, and the smile left a lingering warmth in
his eyes.

'Come and eat,' he said gruffly. 'I take it you aren't
a vegetarian?'

'Well, it is Friday, and a good Catholic girl like
me. . .'

He shot her a searching look. 'Are you serious? I
can easily do you something else.'

She relented. 'One thing I'm not is a good Catholic
girl,' she confessed with a smile. 'I'm under constant
pressure from the family to settle down and raise a
huge brood, but the thought just leaves me cold.'

He looked at her oddly. 'You should. You've got the
right balance of humour and affection, and that wonderful warm openness. You'd be a terrific mother.'

She looked up, startled. 'I'd make a terrible
mother — I have no interest at all in giving up my career
to change nappies.'

'There's rather more to it than that,' he said with a
vain attempt at lightness.

She frowned at him. 'Have you got children?'

That strange thing happened to his face again, the
look she was beginning to recognise and dread.

'No,' he said shortly, and walked away from her
back to the barbecue.

Oh, well. Two steps forward, three back.

She followed him and sniffed appreciatively. 'Smells
delicious. What is it?'

'Chicken tikka. Can you keep an eye on it while I
fetch the salads?'

'Sure. Anything I can do?'

He shook his head. 'What can I get you to drink?'

'Oh, just something soft, I have to drive later.'

'Mineral water?'

She nodded and watched him walk away. He was wearing jeans, like her, and a sweatshirt, and she almost laughed. They were both dressed the same, probably for the same reason, and yet it didn't seem to make any difference because all the action was in the eyes. Every time he looked at her, she came alive inside — except when he got that look, and then a little something died.

Patience, she counselled herself, and turned the chicken in the nick of time.

It was nine o'clock and they had been driven in by the mosquitoes before he broached the subject of the night before.

They were standing in the kitchen loading the dishwasher and putting the salads in the fridge when a picture caught her eye. It was a drawing, a crude pencil sketch of a person, untidily coloured in, in a simple pine frame, with the word 'Daddy' in bold writing beside the figure. It was hanging on the wall in the sitting-room but she hadn't seen it the night before.

For all its amateurish lack of style, it was vigorous and full of life, and she felt instantly drawn to it.

She waved a knife at it. 'Who drew that?'

He glanced up, and she instantly felt she was losing him again.

'My son.'

Here we go, she thought. Very carefully, very deliberately, she set the knife down on the worktop.

'I see.'

'Do you?'

'Well, no, not really. Tell me, Jack — talk to me, for God's sake.'

He nodded, and reaching out for her hand, he led her through into the sitting-room and sat down with her on the settee opposite the picture.

Then he began to talk, very quietly, in a curiously flat voice that showed her more clearly than anything else could how much he was holding back.

'His name was John. He was born sixteen years ago, and we realised that first winter that there was something wrong. I was doing my SHO in paediatrics at the time, and I had a word with my boss. He took one look at him, ran a battery of tests and told us he had cystic fibrosis.'

Kathleen closed her eyes. Now it all fell into place, the child Anthony Craven and his physio that Jack had done so competently, the way he had reacted. . .

'. . .anyway, with time it was obvious that he was going to need more maintenance than Gwen was prepared to give him. I came home from the hospital one day to find Johnnie all alone and desperate for physio, lying on the sitting-room floor crying his eyes out and starving hungry. There was a note from Gwen to say she couldn't take any more. She wanted other children, and by then I'd taken the decision never to have any more and had a vasectomy. We'd rowed about it endlessly, but I was quite determined. Evidently so was she. We heard nothing more from her, except through solicitors, and after the divorce was final, there was nothing.'

'What, *ever*?'

He shook his head. 'Not a word, not in all those years.'

'How old was he?'

'Not quite two.'

She could feel the tears pricking at the back of her eyes. 'Dear God, how could anyone do that?'

Jack shrugged. 'Lord knows. Anyway, I rang my boss, took some time off and my mother and father instantly took over, bless them. We moved in with them, although it meant I had a long journey to the hospital every day and I had to sleep there when I was on call, and we stayed with them until he was nine. He still spent every holiday with them, but I felt he needed more independence and so did they. Mum was getting on by this time and her own health wasn't excellent, and I moved to Manchester so we could be near the RMCH where they do a vast amount with CF. We hired a retired nurse to act as housekeeper and she did his physio when I wasn't there, and between us we managed to keep him going.'

He paused, and she waited, dreading the rest.

'Despite the aggressive treatment and the rigorous fitness programme we set up, he began to deteriorate. He got a chronic pseudomonas infection low down in his lungs, and he was having longer and longer spells in hospital. We'd talked about a heart-lung transplant, and he was on the list, but they never found a suitable match. He died three years ago. He was just thirteen.'

He fell silent, staring broodingly at the picture, and Kathleen closed her eyes to stop the tears from overflowing.

It's the finality of it. . .no matter how prepared you think you are. . . Poor man. Poor, poor, man.

She heard the hiss of a cigarette lighter, and opened

her eyes. He was leaning back, his eyes still fixed on the picture, and his cheeks were wet.

'I still miss him,' he said quietly. 'He was such a vital force in my life, and when he was gone, he took so much of me with him. I'd always known he was going to die, and so had he, really, but when it happened — it was a long time before I could really face it. I thought I'd come to terms with it, but that little lad yesterday. . .'

He rolled his head towards her. 'You just got caught in the crossfire. I'm sorry.'

She lifted her hand and touched his cheek, still damp where the tears had tracked, and bit her lip hard to hold back her own tears.

'I don't know what to say.'

'Don't say anything. Just let me hold you.'

He dropped the cigarette into the ashtray and held out his arms, and she snuggled into them and slipped her hands round behind him, hugging him tight.

She wasn't sure when the wordless comfort changed, or even if it did. Perhaps it just grew and matured until it took in all their emotions, but his hands began to smooth her back and shoulders, until in the end his fingers were threaded through her hair and his big, warm hands were holding her steady while he kissed her with mesmerising thoroughness.

She whimpered and shifted against him, and instantly he released her and straightened away from her with a ragged sigh.

'I'm sorry, I didn't mean to do that.'

She felt bereft, but a part of her still sane enough to try for self-preservation pulled her away from him and drew a deep breath.

'I suppose I ought to go home.'

'That might be wise.' His voice was husky, rough with passion, and scraped over her nerve-endings, leaving her tingling.

She stood up and walked to the door, not trusting herself to look back, and after a second she heard him come to his feet.

'I'll see you to your car,' he said gruffly, and followed her out, opening the car door and closing it after her deliberately.

She wound the window down. 'Are you going in over the weekend?' she asked, already missing the contact. She could feel the defences going up again, brick by brick, but there was no way of breaching them.

'No, I'm going away. I'll be in on Monday.'

The last brick slammed into place. Lifting his hand in a casual salute, he stepped back, leaving her no choice but to start the car and drive away with a casual wave. She made her way through the village and out the other side, then pulled over into a gateway by a field and cried her eyes out.

His defences might be intact, but hers were in ruins, laid waste by a man she hardly knew and yet loved with all her heart.

CHAPTER FOUR

KATHLEEN had always known, deep down, that one day she would meet someone she loved more than her career and would be ready to settle down with him to raise a family.

Now, with one of those obscene little twists that fate was so good at, the man chosen for her out of all those available millions not only couldn't give her children, but had no intention of getting involved in any permanent relationship, least of all marriage!

She had doubts, in fact, that he would even get involved in anything as routine as an affair! At least, not one with any possibility of being taken for granted.

It was a week before he even suggested they get together again for a drink, and that was lunchtime on Friday, at the end of his second week.

It was the usual Friday get-together, the alcohol-free lager and prawn salad session in the pub over the road, well within range of bleeps and so heavily attended by relays of medical and senior nursing staff. As such it hardly qualified as a date, but try telling her heart that!

She went, despising herself for her eagerness and unable to contain it, and watched the charismatic and social side of Jack at work with his colleagues.

He was a brilliant raconteur, with a wicked wit and a razor tongue, and he had them all in stitches. So different from the brooding and unhappy man of a week ago.

Would the real Jack Lawrence please stand up? she thought, and then smiled to herself ruefully. Both were sides of him, of course, not mutually exclusive, and only a fraction of the many-faceted man with whom she had fallen in love.

So she watched, and listened, and fell a little further, and when his bleep went she went back with him to the department and they worked side by side, communicating with a gesture or a word almost in silence, each anticipating the other's needs as they dealt with a little girl who had fallen out of a tree and broken both arms and one leg.

She saw other sides of him then, the skilled physician, the considerate colleague, and yet another side, the one gentle with their frightened little patient, reassuring and comforting her so that the procedures became less terrifying and more easily coped with. The patient stabilised and dispatched to Theatre, he tugged off his mask and grinned.

'We make a good team,' he said, and she glowed with pride and happiness.

She was screwing up the courage to suggest she cook him a meal over the weekend when he glanced at his watch.

'Ben's here, isn't he? Think I'll make a move. I have to get to Yorkshire tonight.'

'Yorkshire?'

He nodded. 'I'm pot-holing tomorrow.'

Her heart plummeted with the thought that he would be away again, and then hitched to a halt when his words registered.

'Pot-holing?' She controlled the squeak in her voice, and tried again. 'Isn't that dangerous?'

He grinned. 'Only if you're stupid. It's fascinating. I've got some fantastic pictures—I'll show you some time. Right, I'll just find Ben and then I'm off.'

She spent the weekend reading books on caving—or more correctly, she discovered, speleology—and it did nothing to set her mind at rest.

'Nuts!' she concluded, regarding a photograph of a filthy caver in wet-suit and helmet, wedged in a muddy slit about two inches thinner than he was. The slit was euphemistically called a squeeze.

She shuddered. What a way to die, stuck between two muddy rocks hundreds of feet under ground. She turned the page. There was a photo of a man dangling on the end of a hundred metres of rope, demonstrating SRT—single rope technique. One bit of string. 'Nuts,' she said again, and tossed the book to one side.

'Why did I have to fall for a suicidal maniac?' she asked herself, and cleaned the flat from top to bottom to take her mind off the image of Jack dangling on the end of a rope above a muddy slit somewhere in subterranean Yorkshire!

He was back on Monday, with a graze on one cheek and perky as a parrot. Perversely, she was cross with him for having survived when she had spent the weekend fretting. To cover the fact that she had far too many feelings altogether, she ignored him for the first part of the morning.

He collared her in the staff-room at eleven-thirty.

'Morning, beautiful. Good weekend?'

'Lovely, thanks,' she lied. 'You?'

'Great—superb conditions. I ache a bit—there were two quite long pitches to climb down, and getting back up is always harder!' He took a swallow of coffee and pulled a face. 'God, this stuff is disgusting. Is your car here?'

She nodded.

'Can we nip down to the catering suppliers at lunchtime and get a decent machine? I'd go, but the bike's still full of ropes and stuff from the weekend and I might not get it in.'

'You went on the bike?' she all but shrieked. 'To Yorkshire?'

'Of course! That's what it's for — speed, freedom and flexibility — and a hell of a lot of fun!'

And that just about sums you up, she thought wryly as the mischievous dimple came and went with his grin, but she wisely said nothing.

They bought a coffee machine at lunchtime, and it was an instant hit with all the passing staff who were called into the department during the course of the day.

'So, who's going to pay for the coffee?' she asked drily as she recharged the filter yet again during the afternoon.

He shrugged. 'I will — damn it, it's worth it. That other stuff was neat toxic waste!'

She wrinkled her nose at him and topped up the reservoir. 'Hmm. We survived on it for years.'

'Yes, well, you're obviously made of sterner stuff than me. It would kill me inside a month!'

'I doubt it — not if biking and pot-holing haven't got you yet. You must have a charmed life.'

He grinned. 'Just exciting. Calculated risks, appropriate safety measures, good equipment. It's like hang-gliding——'

'Like what?' she asked, her heart sinking.

'Hang-gliding — you know, when you — '

' — chuck yourself off a cliff in a pair of paper wings — crazy.'

'Hardly paper, and not usually off cliffs. Anyway, it's fun. Tremendously exhilarating, soaring above the countryside, free as a bird — '

'Yes, well, if God had meant people to fly — '

' — he would have given them wings. You should be good at it.'

She wrinkled her brow. 'Hmm?'

'Flying,' he explained, 'since you're chicken,' and ducking her fist, he left, flapping his elbows and squawking.

'I'll give you chicken, Jack Lawrence,' she muttered laughingly, and followed him out.

The following afternoon he invited her round for another meal. 'I could show you those caving photos,' he said, and she shuddered.

'Are you mad? Why should I want to look at pictures of you stuck in little cracks? No, thanks.'

His face closed up. 'Oh, well, perhaps another time.'

He turned and went back into his office, and she followed him hastily. 'Jack, wait! I didn't mean no to the meal — just to the photos of the caves. It gives me the creeps, that's all. I'd rather not see what you get up to underground.'

His face cleared, and his mouth tipped in a lop-sided grin. 'It's not so bad, really. Some of the caves are beautiful, but you don't have to look at them if you don't want to. It was just an excuse. I thought if I invited you round without one you'd say no.'

She looked up at him in amazement. 'Why should I do that?'

'Why?' He gave a low grunt of laughter. 'Perhaps a little common sense, after the first time?'

She flushed at the memory of their earlier intimacy, and laughed a little self-consciously. 'Oh, come on, Jack, we both know that was a one-off.'

'Was it?' he said softly.

'Yes,' she said firmly. 'I know you now, don't forget. You've got far too much integrity.'

'So what happened that time?'

She reached up and brushed the graze on his cheek. 'You were hurting, and I pushed you.'

'You didn't have to push very hard,' he reminded her, 'but you have my word, nothing will happen that you don't initiate.'

She laughed a little breathlessly. 'That's called passing the buck, Lawrence.'

He grinned wolfishly. 'Of course — there's always the chance you'll drop it! Seven-thirty?'

She answered his grin. 'OK.'

There was a tap on the door. Amy Winship stood there, all but wringing her hands.

'There's a person here who says he's taken an overdose. I didn't know what to do.'

'Fine — thanks, Amy, we'll deal with it. Put him in the wet treatment-room.'

They followed her out.

Their patient was a man in his late thirties, and Kathleen recognised him immediately with a sinking heart. He was a Valium addict who would try anything to obtain a supply of the drug — including pretending to overdose himself so he would be referred to psychiatry. Unfortunately for him, almost all the staff were on to him.

She turned to Jack. 'Leave this to me,' she said under her breath, and winked. Then she turned back to her patient.

'Hello, Jerry. Gone and done it again, have you, old son?'

He nodded and started to cry helplessly.

'It won't work, you know, and you know what I've got to do?'

He nodded and sniffed wetly. Kath sighed. 'Come on, then,' she said kindly, 'let's get you sorted out.' She tugged on a gown and gloves, and reached for the lavage tube, lubricating it. 'Lie down, my love, and open wide. That's lovely—swallow for me—well done.'

She deftly fed the tube down into his stomach, ignoring his gagging protestations, while Amy, following her instructions, filled two jugs with warm water and poured some down the funnel.

Kathleen was just lowering the end over the bucket when Jerry coughed and shot the entire contents of his stomach across the room—and all over her.

Behind her she heard a splutter of laughter, and turned with a glower to see Jack's retreating back.

Amy was biting her lip and trying not to laugh.

'Get a sample for analysis, please,' Kathleen instructed crossly, and with economy of movement she drained the tube, refilled it and flushed several times until the water was clear, and then withdrew the tube.

'There you go, Jerry. Now go home, be a good lad and don't do it again!'

'Can't I have some Valium, Sister?' he grovelled.

'No, you can't,' she told him firmly. 'Now out, please, so I can get cleaned up.'

'Sorry about that. . .' He waved vaguely at the room.

'Jerry, just go home and don't do it again.'

'I won't, Sister, I promise,' he lied.

Amy helped him up and showed him to the door while Kath stripped off her gown and gloves. She came back in, looked at Kath and her mouth twitched.

It wasn't a smart move. 'Get this place cleaned up, Amy, please,' Kathleen said firmly, and had the satisfaction of seeing the girl's face fall.

'Oh, yuck. . .'

Kath relented and grinned wryly. 'You should try wearing it! The frustrating thing is, he probably hadn't taken anything anyway.' She sniffed and grimaced. 'Shower, I think,' she muttered, and went out into the corridor. Jack was coming towards her, and flattened himself against the other side.

'You smell wonderful,' he said with a grin.

'Thank you.' Her smile was saccharine-sweet. 'And thank you for your help in there.'

He lifted his hands in a Gallic shrug. '"Leave this to me," you said.' His eyes tracked to her white lace cap, and the evil grin danced in his eyes. 'Um, Irish?'

She sighed. 'Yes?'

'You've got carrots in your frilly.'

There was nothing in reach to throw at him, unfortunately. With a wicked wink he ducked into the nearest cubicle, safely out of reach.

Torn between tears and laughter, she found herself a clean dress and frilly hat in her locker and went into the showers. One look at her reflection and laughter won.

* * *

'You're a cruel man,' she told him later, putting on a mournful face. 'Fancy laughing at a woman in that condition!'

'I thought the carrots suited you,' he said mildly. 'What with the red hair and all ——'

'What red hair?'

'The red hair you ought to have.' He ducked automatically and grinned. 'What can I get you to drink?'

'Humph. I don't know why I waste time with you, really I don't. Could I have a white wine spritzer?'

He poured her a glass of white wine and tonic, plopped in two ice cubes and slid it over the worktop to her. He was standing in the kitchen, and she was in the living-room the other side of the units. She looked around her appreciatively.

'You've done a lot since I was last here.'

'Oh, not really. Just put up a few pictures and so on. I suppose I ought to organise some curtains, but I never shut them so it's hardly a priority. I'm not exactly overlooked.'

He walked round the end of the units and held out his hand. 'Come and sit down for a minute while the lasagne finishes cooking.'

He sat on the settee and tugged her down beside him, leaning over and sniffing her hair. 'You smell better, anyway.'

'Pig. A gentleman wouldn't have commented,' she told him sternly.

'Of course not, but then you know I'm no gentleman.'

He smiled, and then their eyes clashed and held.

She looked away first, her heart pounding. 'I won't be accused of leading you astray again,' she warned softly, and after a second he chuckled and relaxed back against the settee.

'Aw, shucks,' he said, and she giggled.

'Idiot. Where are these photos, then?'

'But you didn't want to see them.'

'Lady's privilege. I've changed my mind.'

'You're just trying to distract me.'

She grinned. 'Got it in one.'

With an elaborate sigh he unravelled his legs and stood up, crossing the room and squatting down by a pine dresser. He opened a door in the base and pulled out a huge stack of albums.

'Good grief—are they all caves?'

He laughed. 'No—there are lots of Johnnie. I never got round to showing you the photos of him last time.'

He showed her the caving ones first, and then they paused for supper before going back to look at the ones of his son.

Kathleen was worried that it would upset him, but he seemed quite relaxed, laughing over incidents and reminiscing out loud. The only low point was the last album, with a photo of his son in hospital. For the first time the laughter was extinguished from the little face so like Jack's, and in its place was resignation and courage, and a wisdom far beyond his years.

'I love that photo,' Jack said softly. 'I've got an enlargement of it in the bedroom. It was the last photo I took of him. He died early the following morning.' On the facing page, out of sequence, was an earlier photo of Johnnie laughing, his head thrown back, radiating life and energy. 'Whenever I get the blues, I look at this,' Jack murmured, his finger tracing the contours of his son's face. 'It reminds me that although his death was tragic, his life was full of fun and laughter. We had so many good times. No one can ever take that away from us.'

He sat quietly for a while, staring into space, and then abruptly shut the album and stood up. 'Walk?'

Not quite touching, they strolled down the drive to the lane and then along a little way to where a stream meandered under a little bridge. They stood on the bridge listening to the chuckling water, and after a moment Jack drew Kathleen into his arms.

'Will you scream if I kiss you?' he murmured softly.

In answer she lifted herself up on tiptoe and leaned against his tall, firm frame.

With a soft sigh his head came down and he took her lips in a gentle, lingering kiss. After a moment she moved away, her heart pounding. It would be so easy. . .

'I must go home,' she said, and her voice sounded strangled in the quiet night.

He squeezed her hand in understanding, and walked her back to her car.

'Thank you for a lovely evening,' she said, now strangely reluctant to leave.

'My pleasure,' he murmured, and for a second they stood there, regarding each other watchfully, the tension straining between them.

Only too conscious of the depth of passion simmering in him, and conscious too of her crumbling resistance and his vow that nothing would happen that she didn't initiate, she took a deep, shaky breath and got into the car, shutting the door firmly behind her.

He squawked and flapped his wings, and the tension

dissolved in their shared laughter. 'You're a wicked man,' she said fondly. 'Goodnight, Jack.'

His smile was wry and full of understanding. 'Goodnight, Irish. See you tomorrow.'

She didn't trust herself to say anything else. With a smile, she started the car and drove swiftly away.

In fact it was Jack's sense of humour that kept her feelings in proportion during the next few days. Whenever the tension mounted, he defused it with a razor-edged comment, as often as not directed at himself, and so they were able to keep the rising tide of passion at bay.

Kathleen knew it was only a case of stalling for time, but every day that passed brought new understanding of this enigmatic man who had captured her heart.

He still irritated her with his casual dress, the sloppy tie hanging round his neck, the top button always undone, the lazy grin and teasing remarks in front of her colleagues, but as he teased them all she was in no way singled out. In fact, if he hadn't teased her, it would have been more obvious that there was some undercurrent in their communication with each other.

Professionally, though, she never had any cause to doubt his judgement or medical skill. He was fast, intuitive and decisive, his movements clean and minimal, his manner reassuring.

He often cracked jokes with patients to relax them, his easy camaraderie taking the edge off their fear without in any way compromising their faith in him.

It was the way she liked to work, and, watching him, she realised he was a master at it. Not only a master, but a natural comedian, because he found humour in seemingly impossible situations.

His wit was never cruel, but it was always horribly accurate and often wicked. Just how wicked she didn't realise until the next weekend, when she was on nights covering the regular night sister who was on holiday. Jack was on call, and they were passing the wee small hours of Saturday morning in idle conversation when the phone rang in the staff-room.

It was an unusually quiet night, and Jack had been called in earlier and had stayed not out of necessity but because, as he said, if he went home he would only be called out again.

Kathleen answered the phone, listened for a minute and asked a few questions, and then cradled the receiver with a groan. Jack's brow arched in enquiry, and she shrugged.

'Woman with a heavy period, demanding to see a gynaecologist before she bleeds to death. There's only one problem.'

'Which is?'

The receptionist thinks she's a man.'

An imp of mischief danced in Jack's eyes. 'Is that a fact? Well, well. . .'

He rose lazily to his feet and sauntered out into the corridor. 'Coming, Irish? I think this could be rather fun.'

'Oh, my lord,' she muttered, and followed him.

The 'lady' in question was heavily made up and dressed in a tight sheath of black and gold lurex that ended provocatively at mid-thigh. Her hairstyle was a bizarre pile of curls heaped somewhat haphazardly on the top of her head, and she was crouched over her stomach, clutching it most convincingly. The most remarkable feature, in fact, was the enormous pair of high-heeled shoes at the end of the spangled tights.

'Good legs,' Jack commented appreciatively. 'This could be a real lulu.' He leant over the receptionist. 'That geezer in the dress — what's his name?'

She looked down at the computer screen. 'Queenie Butcher.'

There was a stifled snort of laughter from Jack, and Kathleen bit the inside of her cheek.

'Jack, you can't. . .'

'Watch me. Mrs Butcher, please,' he said clearly, and the creature rose to her feet.

'Ms Butcher, if you don't mind,' she simpered.

'I do beg your pardon — Mizz Butcher — would you come with me, please?'

Kathleen restrained the urge to roll her eyes as Jack led 'Queenie' to the little theatre at the back of A and E.

'Right, lie down on the couch and answer a few of these questions, and we'll see what we can do for you. When did your problems start?'

How he kept a straight face Kath would never know. She turned her back to him and fiddled with a trolley, and bit her cheek till it bled. Finally he ground to a halt and stood up.

'Right, Sister Hennessy, if you could prepare Queenie — you don't mind if we call you Queenie? Good — for a gynaecologist, I'll get Reception to page one for us. I think the lithotomy stirrups, please.'

And he left her to it!

Calling on an acting ability not required since her childhood, she covered her patient with a cotton blanket and then hitched up each leg in turn and strapped them into the lithotomy stirrups, thus trapping the hoaxer until the joke had run its course.

She went out and found Jack at the nursing station with Jake Hunter, the obs and gynae senior registrar.

'All set, Irish?' Jack asked her.

She gave a disbelieving laugh. 'Well, I did as you said.'

'Excellent. Come on then, Jake, let's give him a fright.'

'You are quite sure about this?' Jake asked dubiously, running a hand through his dark, floppy hair. 'I mean, I would hate to find she really was ——'

'She really isn't, Jake,' Kathleen assured him. 'Not unless she's had a very nasty prolapse!'

He chuckled. 'OK. I'm game if you are. It's a shame Annie isn't on — a woman would be even better.'

Jack laughed. 'Come on, let's find out how far he's prepared to carry this through.'

But he wasn't. When they went back in, 'Queenie' was struggling to get his second leg out of the lithotomy stirrups.

Jack laid a firm hand over his shin and held him there effortlessly. 'What's the matter, Queenie?' he asked, his voice a river of silken reassurance. 'We won't hurt you. Why are you running away?'

In desperation he tugged of his wig and looked pleadingly at them. 'Look, it was just a gag, OK? No harm done, or anything — I had a bet with a friend that I couldn't con you.'

Jack grinned. 'Tell your friend he was right. You didn't even get past the receptionist, but I like the gear. Very pretty.'

Queenie almost preened. 'Well thanks, duckie. It's my show gear — I sing at a gay club in town. Any time you're passing, come in and have a drink. You never know,' his eyes ran over Jack's body lingeringly, 'maybe I could even be persuaded. . .'

Jack chuckled. 'Thanks for the compliment, but no, thanks. My current's strictly AC. For the record — ' he released the leg and Queenie straightened up in relief ' — I could call the police and have you arrested for wasting NHS resources on a hoax, but I tell you what, I'll settle for a donation to the Cystic Fibrosis Research Trust.' He grinned like a crocodile. 'Just to show how nice I really am.'

The man slipped off the couch, wriggled his feet into his enormous high-heeled shoes and tugged his wig on. 'Done. Here — ' He rummaged in the pearl-studded evening bag and came up with a twenty pound note. 'Can I leave it with you?'

Jack plucked it from his fingers and grinned again. 'Most generous. You're too kind.'

'Any time, duckie.' Straightening his skirt, Queenie sauntered out, turning at the entrance to wink saucily at Jack.

He returned the wink, and Kathleen closed her eyes in despair.

'Mr Lawrence, you should be reported for demanding money with menaces.'

He slung an arm around her shoulders and grinned at Jake. 'Coffee?'

'I gather you've got a new machine.'

'Word travels,' Kath said drily. 'I'd better fill it up.'

* * *

They were still talking about the incident on Wednesday when Kathleen returned to work after her days off.

'Wish I'd seen it,' Ben Bradshaw said mournfully. 'Nothing like that ever happens to me. All I get is the blood and guts.'

'Ah, poor boy,' Kath teased. 'Never mind, there's a nice toenail in cubicle three you can go and remove to cheer you up.'

He wrinkled his nose fastidiously. 'Clean feet?'

She chuckled. 'Shouldn't think so — you don't get that lucky! Amy Winship's in there — she'll help you.'

He sighed and ambled down the corridor, whistling 'Hi-ho, hi-ho,' under his breath.

Kathleen went back into her office and found Jack in there, slouched in her chair with a cup of coffee in his hand. She took it from him and drained the cup.

'Lovely — thanks.'

He laughed and tugged her on to his lap. 'I was enjoying that — you'll have to pay for it.'

She squirmed and his arms clamped tighter. 'Don't do that, Irish, it's bad for my blood pressure,' he murmured in her ear. 'Now come on, pay up like a good little girl.'

She levered herself away from him with a hand on his chest and looked him dead in the eye. 'You don't want a good little girl, Jack Lawrence —— '

'Oh, I do, but she won't co-operate.'

She froze for a second, caught by the magnetic intensity of those granite eyes, and beneath her palm she could feel the heavy beat of his heart.

The moment seemed destined to stretch on endlessly, but then there was a sharp tap at the door followed by a gasp of embarrassment.

'I'm sorry — I ——'

She leapt to her feet and turned round, fighting the blush. 'It's all right, Amy. Mr Lawrence was just going ——' She shoved his feet off her desk and glared at him.

He unwound himself and stood up, grinned unrepentantly at them both and sauntered out.

Amy watched him go with her jaw dangling, then turned back to Kathleen.

'Um — Dr Bradshaw wondered if you could come. He growled something about my septic technique.'

'Septic or aseptic?'

She shifted uncomfortably. 'He said septic.'

Kathleen groaned. 'All right, Amy. I'll go through it with you again.'

Ben was right, Kath thought later. Amy's technique was abysmal. She carted all the junior nursing staff off during the afternoon for a training session in one of the treatment-rooms, and by the end of a vigorous drilling they seemed to have it firmly implanted. She just hoped it stayed there.

The other reason she had disappeared with the juniors was that it kept her out of Jack's way. Just as well for him, because she was hopping mad.

She saw him later going into his office and followed him.

'You ——' she began, levelling a finger at him, and he chuckled and tugged her into his arms.

'Sorry, sweetheart.'

'Don't sorry sweetheart me! You're doing it again! Now put me down and for goodness' sake behave!'

He released her and stood back, eyeing her thought-fully. 'You really are cross, aren't you?'

'Cross doesn't begin to cover it,' she told him furiously. 'Do you have any idea how embarrassing it is to be caught *in flagrante* with my boss?'

'*In flagrante*?' he laughed incredulously. 'My dear girl, you were sitting on my lap!'

She sniffed disapprovingly, and earned a chuckle for her pains.

'Oh, Irish, you are so lovely when you're mad——'

'Don't patronise me!' she stormed. 'I have worked very hard in this hospital to earn the respect of my colleagues, and in one fell swoop you've managed to compromise my integrity——'

'Hang on in there a minute, my lovely. I have done nothing—absolutely nothing!—to compromise your professional integrity, or to lose you the respect of your colleagues. All I've done is dent your holier-than-thou force-field a little bit. Lighten up, old thing. Why shouldn't we have a relationship?'

And that was the trouble, of course.

She looked up at him slowly. 'No reason at all, but we haven't, have we?'

After a second or two, he looked away. 'No. You're right. I'm sorry I embarrassed you.'

He was polite but distant after that for the rest of the week, and there was no suggestion that they should get together in the evening or over the weekend.

She was in one of the cubicles tidying up on Monday morning when he limped in.

'Hi.' He grinned sheepishly. 'Got a minute?'

'Of course—what have you done?'

'Hang-gliding — bit of an awkward landing. I often do it, but this time was a bit worse.'

She sighed. 'Let me see — sit on the couch and pull up your trouser leg. I hope your feet are clean?'

'Damn cheek,' he muttered, and hitched himself up onto the edge of the couch.

Very carefully she eased off his shoe and sock. 'Hmm,' she said enigmatically.

'Hmm yourself. What about poor old thing, let me give you a bit of TLC?'

'TLC yourself,' she snorted. 'Don't expect sympathy. Anyone daft enough to chuck themselves off a cliff —'

He squawked and flapped his arms, and she slapped his leg. 'Shut up and sit still. Do you want Tubigrip on it or not?'

'Yes, please, Sister. Sorry, Sister.'

She glared at him and he winked wickedly. 'I love it when you're rough with me,' he said huskily. 'Hit me again.'

'Jack, would you for God's sake shut up or I'll get Amy Winship and Joe Reynolds to come and deal with you!'

He shuddered and clapped a hand over his mouth, rolling his eyes theatrically.

She ignored him with difficulty and threaded a length of Size C Tubigrip on to the frame and then up over his ankle. 'There — how's that?'

'Tight.'

'It's meant to be.'

'So it is. Thank you, you're an angel.'

'Don't grovel, it doesn't become you.'

He laughed despairingly. 'What can I do? I'm not allowed to do what comes naturally ——'

'Which is what?'

'This. . .' He reached out and tugged her into the V of his thighs, dropping his mouth to hers and taking it in a kiss that left her gasping for breath and so shaken she could barely stand.

She eased away and touched her fingers to her lips. 'You shouldn't have done that,' she breathed raggedly.

'You see? I can't win.' He slid off the couch, put on his sock and shoe carefully and limped out, leaving her slumped against the couch in despair.

It was another uneasy week, and by Friday afternoon she was longing for the end of the shift so she could go home and wallow in misery.

She went into the empty staff-room and helping herself to a cup of coffee, she sank wearily into a chair.

'Tired?'

She jumped and nearly slopped hot coffee over her skirt. 'Not really.' She watched as he crossed the room. He was still limping slightly, but much less than at the beginning of the week.

'Well, what is it this weekend?' she asked rashly, before her mouth came under control from her brain. 'Crawling down holes, or chucking yourself off cliffs?'

'Camping.'

'*Camping*?' she exclaimed.

He shrugged. 'The ankle needs to settle before I can go caving or flying again. I thought I'd go off and have a look at the north Norfolk coast, up near Blakeney.'

'Oh, it's lovely up there,' she said wistfully. 'You'll enjoy it.'

He hesitated a second, then met her eyes. 'Come with me.'

'What?'

'You heard.'

Her heart was pounding, her mouth dry. She knew what he was asking, and she knew what her answer would be.

'When do we leave?'

He grinned. 'Five tonight. And travel light—we're going on the bike.'

CHAPTER FIVE

BY A quarter to five Kathleen was having serious doubts about her sanity.

The inevitability of the next step in her relationship with Jack faded into insignificance compared with the sheer terror she was experiencing at the thought of going on his bike.

'I should have said no,' she muttered, looking yet again at the tiny pile of things she had accumulated. Were they suitable? Were jeans and T-shirt the right thing to wear, and what about her feet? Were trainers OK? She would need them over the weekend, God willing. Would they even get there? And what about a helmet?

She closed her eyes and dropped on to the bed, her heart pounding. Her hands were shaking, the palms damp, and she knew she couldn't stand to save her life. Every week there was a succession of motorbike accidents through the department, many serious, some fatal — she must be insane.

Suddenly she couldn't sit still any longer, and jumping up, she paced to the window of her sitting-room and peered out. Did she have time to run away? What if he hadn't left yet — she could ring him and tell him she'd chickened out, and he could flap his wings and tease her but at least she wouldn't have to — oh, hell, here he is, she thought, and watched as the huge bike rolled to a halt and he switched off the engine and hauled it up on the stand. It looked enormous, sleek and very, very fast.

I can't do it, she thought frantically, and then the bell was ringing and she had no choice but to open the door.

His face clouded instantly with concern. 'Are you OK? You're as white as a sheet.'

'Fine,' she said shortly. 'I'm all ready.'

He handed her a bag. 'Try these. They're my old leathers from way back when I was skinny. The jeans'll be a bit long and the jacket'll drown you, but at least you'll be protected a bit if we come off—oh, and I've got a lid for you to try. Hang on.'

If we come off, she thought despairingly. Lord, how can he be so casual about it?

He went back to the bike and unlocked one of the panniers, coming back with a colourful helmet. 'Here. Try it.'

She took it in shaking fingers and pulled it on, immediately feeling very closed in by the visor. He took her head in his hands and rocked the helmet, but it didn't move. He nodded his satisfaction and let go, and she wrenched it off and took a deep breath.

'No good? Is it too tight?'

'It's the thing over my face—I feel I can't breathe!'

'It's ventilated—here, look.' He showed her the little holes in the chin guard, and reluctantly she tried it again. He was right, she could breathe, but only if she closed her eyes so she couldn't see the perspex two inches from her nose!

She took it off again. 'OK. Let me go and try the leather stuff on. What else do I need?'

'Jeans, sweatshirt, shorts, undies, wash things—not

much. Have you got any boots? Knee-length leather ones, ideally.'

She frowned doubtfully. 'Winter fashion boots, with a low heel — will they do?' At his nod, she took the bag and went into her bedroom, pulling off her denim jeans and wriggling into the leather ones. They were loose around the waist and the legs seemed endless, but the hips fitted nice and snugly. The jacket was huge, but again fitted well around the hips and the cuffs had ajustable snap-fasteners. At least if she fell off she wouldn't lose all her skin —

'How're you doing?'

She opened the door, and he ran a critical eye over her before nodding. 'You'll do. Where's your stuff?'

She showed him the tiny pile on the bed, and he nodded again. 'Good. You're the first woman I've ever met who had the slightest idea what travelling light means. Right, sit down on the bed and give me your legs.'

She did as she was told, and with surgical precision he slashed four inches off the legs of the jeans. 'There.' He folded the knife again and slid it into a pocket. 'What have you got on under the leather stuff?'

'A T-shirt — '

'Not enough. Find a long jumper that comes well down, and tuck it in so you don't get a draught over your kidneys. I'll pack your stuff into the bike.'

He left the room and she tugged on a sweater and put the jacket back on just as he came back in.

'All set?'

She nodded.

'Right, let's roll.'

'What about sleeping-bag and tent and stuff?' she asked, stalling frantically now the time was here.

'On the bike. All I need is you.'

'Well, Jack Lawrence, you old romantic!' she teased with the last remnant of her sense of humour, and he smiled a slow, lazy smile.

'I can be. Come on, then. I want to get there in daylight.'

She followed him out, locking the door and slipping the keys into her handbag. 'Any room for this?'

'Sure.' He squeezed it into one of the panniers, and snapped it shut. 'OK, let's go. Here, I've put an intercom into your helmet, so we can listen to music and if you want to talk to me, you press this button here—OK? Clip this to your jacket.'

He swung his leg over the saddle, rocked the bike off its stand and balanced it with his legs while she put on the helmet, tugged on the huge gloves and tried not to let him know she was panicking.

Suddenly his voice came over the headphones. 'Can you hear me?'

She nodded, and he grinned behind his visor. 'Press the button and say, "Yes, Jack."'

'Yes, Jack,' she mimicked saucily, and he laughed.

'Hop on, then.'

She swallowed and slid her leg over the saddle behind him, and he put her feet on the rests and told her to wrap her arms round him.

She needed no second bidding. She slid up close to his back, wrapped her arms firmly round his waist and tried to relax.

Pointless. He started the bike, eased it forwards and

suddenly they were tilting over as they went round the corner.

Her grip tightened as he accelerated, and after a moment or two he coasted slowly into the kerb and stopped.

'Are you OK?' he asked.

'Um — I'm just scared —— '

'Press the button.'

'Oh. Right. Can you hear me?'

He turned round, took her intercom control in his hand and then gave her another lesson in operating the controls. 'Now,' he said patiently. 'What's wrong?'

She lifted her shoulders in a little shrug. 'I've never done it before.'

'OK. We'll go nice and slowly, and if you really hate it, we'll get my car and take that. OK?'

She nodded, infinitely relieved. Just a few minutes more and she'd be safe.

'OK, now try and relax and hold on to me. I'm not going anywhere — just go with my body.'

She nodded again, and he winked and turned back. Seconds later they were off again, and she shut her eyes tight, pressed her cheek against his back and clung on like a limpet. Soft music flooded through her helmet, and if she ignored the sensation of movement, she could almost pretend she was sitting at home. . . almost.

They headed north, and after a few minutes she began to think she might actually survive. Then they hit the main road and he opened the bike up and for an awful second she thought she was going to slide off the back.

Unthinking, she tightened her grip and felt him laugh under her hands.

His voice replaced the music in the helmet.

'Much as I love being crushed between your thighs, do you think you could leave me a little circulation? It's awfully hard to ride this thing with numb legs!'

Mortified, she released her death-grip on his waist and tried hard to relax her legs.

'Just go with the flow, Irish. There's nothing to it. You never know, you might even enjoy yourself!'

Fat chance, she thought in despair, but little by little, when nothing happened to unsettle her, she was able to relax more and in doing so became aware of all the little things she had missed before — the warmth of his back against her chest, the firm feel of his waist under her hands, the slight shift of his thighs against hers as he changed gear. Even the scenery began to enchant her, and the tug of the wind on her clothes became a pleasure rather than just another instrument of torture.

With a deep sigh, she snuggled against his back and settled down to enjoy the journey.

'You survived.'

She laughed sheepishly. 'I'm sorry — I had no idea I'd be such a dreadful wimp.'

His smile was sympathetic. 'The trouble is you've seen too much. There are too many idiots on the road, and they all end up coming through our department, but provided you're sensible and don't take risks either with yourself or your equipment, you should be OK.'

'Should be.'

He shrugged. 'Nothing's foolproof. Want some more food?'

She shook her head. 'No, I'm fine.' She looked around. They were on a slight hill on the edge of a little copse, and in the distance she could see the lights of boats on the sea. From where they were there wasn't a soul to be seen—certainly no other campers. 'How did you persuade the farmer to let us use his field?' she asked.

'Natural charm.'

She chuckled. Looking at his grin, she could well believe it. 'How much natural charm?'

The grin widened. 'Ten quids' worth.'

'Ten pounds——? But you could go to a campsite for far less!'

He shrugged. 'You want company?'

She shook her head. 'No. . .'

He stood up abruptly. 'I'll get the tent up. I don't think it's going to rain, but it's as well to be on the safe side.'

She frowned in puzzlement. 'Don't you sleep in it anyway?'

'Not if I can help it. It's like being zipped into a sponge bag—yuck. The best part about camping is the fact that you're out in the open. Seems crazy to me to shut yourself in.'

'Want a hand?'

He shook his head. 'You stay there, I'll manage.'

She packed up the remains of the bread and cheese they had had for supper, and then watched as he clipped poles together and hammered in pegs; within minutes the flimsy little structure was up and ready. It looked tiny, no more than an emergency shelter, which of course was all it was intended to be. Her eyes followed him as he unpacked the bike, and she wondered if he was just going to take it for granted that she would sleep with him of if he would offer her the choice.

Now what? he thought frustratedly. Damn it, why had he brought her here? He'd regretted the invitation as soon as the words were out of his mouth. He'd only ever taken Johnnie camping before, and had no idea how she would take to it. Probably scream if an earwig crawled into the sleeping-bag — and that was the other thing. Did he zip them together or just hand her one? Could he assume? Would she or wouldn't she?

Hell, he couldn't even ask, having told her the next time she would have to take the initiative, but if she didn't take it soon he was going to go out of his mind! Every time he looked at her he wanted her more. It wasn't just her body, either, though God knew there was nothing wrong with it. His own tightened in anticipation, and he swore softly under his breath. No, he wanted more than just her body, although what and why he didn't care to analyse. That was part of the reason for his edginess.

She was getting to him, wriggling past his defences and beginning to matter, and that was bad news. Even so, he found he couldn't walk away. Damn, why had he hurt her before? She was so sweet and funny, sharp as a tack and yet never unkind. In fact her only fault was her unrelenting interest in him, and like before he was helpless, devoid of the steely self-denial needed to walk away from her.

But how to tackle it? Last time had been so traumatic; what if he had put her off him for life? She would need such care and gentleness, and if it killed

him he would give it to her, but the passion was raging
in him until he could hardly see straight. He realised
with a shock that he was nervous — as nervous as a
randy adolescent on a hot date — and likely to be about
as subtle!

Damn. He fished a cigarette out of his pocket and
flicked the lighter. The end glowed in the twilight. She
was watching him. What was she thinking? Perhaps he
ought to take her home before he embarrassed both of
them.

He drew deeply on the cigarette and stared out at
the darkening sea. It was late now. He was going to
have to make a move, one way or the other. Perhaps
he would just hand her a sleeping-bag and offer her the
tent. . .

Something was wrong. She didn't know what, but it
wasn't like her to skirt an issue. She watched as he
finished his cigarette, and then turned towards the
bike. She heard him swear softly, and then he limped
a little.

'Is your ankle still sore?'

'Only if I forget and twist it,' he said shortly, and
pulled a groundsheet and two tightly rolled sleeping-
bags out of the pannier. He spread out the groundsheet
and unrolled the sleeping-bags, then paused. She saw
him flex his ankle and wince, and she stood up and
went over to him, kneeling down on the end of one of
the sleeping-bags.

'Sit down, I'll rub it.'

'It's fine,' he said shortly.

'Jack, shut up,' she told him good-naturedly, and
waited as he dropped on to the sleeping-bag.

She unzipped the boot and eased it off, then unzipped the ankle of his leather suit and slid the leg up a little.

'It's swollen again — you haven't been resting it.'

Her fingers were gentle but firm, and he sprawled back on his elbows and watched her as she lifted his foot on to her lap and massaged all the tired muscles.

After a few minutes she bent her head and dropped a kiss lightly on his ankle, and then her hand slid up under the leg of the leathers and sensuously kneaded the firm muscle at the back of his calf.

She heard the sharp hiss of his indrawn breath, and then he bent forwards and drew her gently up into his arms. His breath was warm on her hair, and she could feel the trembling in his arms.

'Irish. . .?'

'I thought you'd never ask,' she whispered, and in the gathering darkness she heard a ragged sigh just before his head came down and blocked out the stars.

His lips were warm and firm and tasted of smoky coffee, and they brushed hers lightly, tormentingly.

She threaded her hands through his hair and kissed him back, and suddenly all the pent-up emotion of the past few weeks rushed up to engulf her.

She whimpered and he gentled the kiss, but it wasn't what she wanted. She arched against him, her hands searching desperately for his skin, and with a harsh groan he stood up and dragged her to her feet.

'Hang on,' he growled, and zipped the two sleeping bags together as fast as he could with shaking hands. Then those hands were unzipping and tugging and peeling off clothes as though they were on fire. Even so, it seemed forever before he drew her back into his arms.

The first contact of skin on skin was electric. His back was smooth and firm, hot under her palms, and the muscles rippled as she slid her hands down and smoothed them over the slight swell of his hips.

His arms went round her and eased her against his chest, and the brush of his body hair against her nipples made her cry out. Their legs tangled, and she cried out again as his thigh grazed between hers and rocked against her. Her lips found the soft skin in the angle of his shoulder, and her tongue dipped into the hollow of his throat, tasting the saltiness of his skin.

She could feel the pounding of his heart against her chest, and the pulse leapt under her lips. One large hand came up and cupped a breast, the thumb grazing one nipple as his head dipped and he drew the other into his mouth, suckling deeply.

A choked sob rose in her throat, and she felt his chuckle as he switched his attention to the other breast.

'Jack, please,' she whimpered, and he diverted his attention lower, stroking and taunting until she thought she would die.

Then he lowered her to the ground and shifted over her, and for a second it was like it had been before and fear touched her, but then his lips came down and brushed her mouth, and she was lost.

Her legs locked round his waist and she arched against him, pleading with him, and slowly, with infinite care, he eased into her.

It wasn't enough. After all this time, she wanted more — much more. He started to move, slowly at first and then faster in response to her pleas, and then suddenly everything disintegrated in a wild starburst of colour and sensation that left her shaken and helpless in his arms.

'Are you OK?'

His voice was gruff in the darkness, and she rolled her head towards him and reached up to touch his face.

'I'm fine — why shouldn't I be?'

He gave a low grunt of laughter, followed by an untidy sigh. 'I thought I might have hurt you — God knows I tried to be careful, but you seem to have this knack of wiping out twenty-five years of control and finesse with a single touch.'

'Twenty-five years? Lord, you started young!'

He chuckled. 'Not really. It was quite legal.'

She propped herself up on one elbow and looked down at his face in the starlight, her mind tangling on the mental arithmetic. 'You can't be forty-one!'

'Almost.'

She dropped back beside him. 'Amazing. You must be like a good wine.'

He chuckled again, and his fingers threaded through hers under the covers. They had taken refuge from the insects and the dew when sanity returned, and were lying gazing up at the stars.

Kathleen turned on her side and snuggled closer, resting her head on his shoulder. Her fingers trailed slowly over his chest, tangling absently in the soft curls. Lord, she loved him. Telling him would be a mistake, she knew that, just as surely as she knew he would never tell her what he really felt, but she knew.

Desire, yes, of course, or they would never have ended up like this, but also a reluctant fascination and a curiously protective tendency that she found both touching and revealing.

That love would come she had no doubt. Whether or not he would ever admit it was a different kettle of fish entirely.

His other hand came over and settled on her waist, the thumb drawing idle circles on her skin.

Turning his head, he brushed his lips against her brow in silent question.

Without hesitation, she lifted her mouth to his.

They woke to blue skies and glorious sunshine. Dressing quickly in shorts and T-shirts, they packed the gear away in the tent and Jack parked the bike in the trees, out of sight.

Then they set off over the fields for the nearest village, two miles away. They bought hot rolls and coffee in the little café, and ate them sitting on the sand dunes overlooking the sea, and then they wandered along the tideline searching for treasures.

Jack found a piece of driftwood, its gnarled form worn totally smooth by the action of the waves, and they decided it would look wonderful in his barn hung on the brickwork chimney-breast, so he carried it for the rest of the morning until they returned to their little camp at lunchtime.

They took the bike then and rode along the coast to Blakeney. They took a boat trip to see the seals, and in the evening they went back to the camp and lit a picnic-type disposable barbecue and ate burgers and sausages and fresh crunchy salad they had bought in Blakeney.

As darkness fell again they took turns to wash in the

tent, and then they lay together under the night sky and reached again for the stars.

She woke in the night to find him lying flat on his back, the glow of a cigarette lighting up his face as he inhaled.

'Can't you sleep?' she asked softly.

He was silent for a long time, then he blew out a long stream of smoke and turned his head towards her.

'Don't fall for me, Irish. This has been a great weekend, but it doesn't mean anything.'

She swallowed the hurt and told herself he didn't really mean it. He just didn't realise he loved her yet.

'Sure, and why would I fall for you?' she asked lightly, staring hard at the stars. If she could just keep them from swimming out of focus. . .

'You said you loved me.'

She was shocked. Had she said it aloud? God knew she'd thought it, but aloud?

'Oh, that,' she said dismissively. 'You don't want to take everything I say too seriously. It's just the heat of the moment. Anyway, I'm a good Catholic girl, remember? I've got to settle down and have babies, so you're quite safe. You're not in the least a suiable candidate.'

The cigarette glowed again in the dark, and he hitched himself up on one elbow and ground it out on the earth.

'No, I'm not,' he growled. 'Just make sure you don't forget it.'

'You're quite good in bed, though,' she added cheekily.

He gave a disbelieving laugh.

'Are you propositioning me?'

'Well, do you know, I believe I might be?'

His arms went round her and his lips found hers, and this time when the world fell apart and the sky came crashing down, she clamped her lips together and buried her face in his shoulder and said nothing.

'Well, you can't say he didn't warn you,' she muttered to herself during the course of Monday. Their 'great weekend' as he put it had come to a highly unsatisfactory end yesterday evening, when he had dropped her off at home, and after seeing her in, had ridden off with scarcely a word. 'Well, he said it didn't mean anything, so you've only got yourself to blame if you didn't believe him,' Kathleen told herself glumly.

Sunday had been wonderful, a lovely warm, lazy day, but since then he had treated her as just another member of the team, being quite natural and friendly and polite, but without any hint of intimacy.

In fact, looking back on it there had been no hint of any real intimacy over the weekend, except during their lovemaking. Then there had been plenty, both physical and emotional, but only then. It was as if that was the only emotion Jack allowed himself, the only time he let down his guard, and she sensed that it was almost involuntary and if he could have prevented it he would have done.

In fact, if anything he was even more remote and distant now than he had been before their weekend, as if he hadn't meant to let her get so close and was frantically clawing back space.

If so, the fates were playing into his hands. They had been busy in the department all day, a steady stream of non-urgent cases that kept her occupied and largely out of his way — until the middle of the afternoon, at any rate. Then a motorcyclist was brought in on a blue light, a dispatch rider who had been burning along the Norwich road and hit a patch of oil.

He was a mess, his left femur broken in at least one place, his right tibia and fibula shattered, his right shoulder dislocated and possible rib fractures.

Thinking of her trip to Norfolk on the back of Jack's bike, Kathleen's blood ran cold.

'Fat lot of use leather gear is to you under these circumstances,' she mumbled, and set to with her scissors to cut away his shredded clothes.

'Can we get the orthopaedic SR on take down here, please?' she threw over her shoulder, and then added, as an afterthought, 'and the neurologist?'

The team went smoothly into action as usual, only Kathleen's racing pulse betraying her inner horror. She wondered how much longer it would be before Jack was brought in in this sort of state, and how she would feel if he was.

Sick, was the short answer.

She made herself smile. 'Hello in there,' she said to him, and he groaned and rolled his head towards her. 'Can you tell me your name?'

'Graham — Glover.'

'Are you in a lot of pain, Graham?'

'Are you kidding?' he gritted.

She nodded. 'I'll get you something in a tick. Did they give you anything in the ambulance?'

'I dunno,' he slurred. 'If they did, it didn't work. . .'

Jack appeared at her elbow, winced and commiserated. 'Soon have you comfortable,' he lied easily. 'Let's have six units of whole blood cross-matched and run in some plasma expander in the meantime. I think Michael Barrington's on his way down now — ah, the very man.'

Jack filled him in on the scanty information they had already obtained.

'Ouch — hello, old chap,' he said with a smile. 'I'm the guy with the job of gluing you together again. Have we got any X-rays?'

'No, he's going in now,' Kathleen said. 'I wasn't sure what you wanted, and I thought it was better to wait and get the whole lot.'

'OK. Let's take things in order — pain relief, X-rays, then we'll get that shoulder back in before we go much further. I think we'll need a full set, actually. I'm not sure if that leg's lying oddly because of the femur or the pelvis.' He turned back to the patient. 'Have you got any pain in your back or hips, Graham?'

He gave a feeble chuckle, and clutched his ribs with his left hand. 'Ow, damn. I don't know where it's coming from, and frankly, I don't give a monkey's.'

'OK. We'll give him seventy-five milligrams of pethidine, get the shots and go from there.'

Kathleen injected the painkiller, and then he was wheeled off for X-rays.

They went into the staff-room and grabbed a coffee while they waited for the results, then they studied them together on the lightbox.

'Ow,' Michael said. 'Better get Theatre jumping, I think. Maybe need a fixator on the tib and fib, or put the right leg in a gutter for a day or two and see. I think I'll probably pin the femur, now we know the pelvis is cracked too. Don't want traction on it.'

Jack grinned at him. 'Another early night?'

He laughed. 'Don't. Clare'll kill me. Still, it's not for much longer, then we're taking two months off to sail the Atlantic.'

Jack did a mild double take. 'Pardon?'

'Don't ask,' Kathleen advised. 'I thought you were bad, but this one's a menace. If it's impossible, he does it. Something to prove to the world, isn't that right, Michael?'

He smiled slowly. 'Well, to myself, perhaps. Still, it's a bit of fun.'

'What have you got?' Jack asked.

'Thirty-eight-foot sloop. My grandfather built her.'

Kathleen glared at Jack. 'You have enough dangerous hobbies,' she muttered.

'What, like the bike?'

She snorted.

'Talking of the bike, let's go and put that shoulder back. You any good at this?'

'Oh, yeah. Nothing like a good dislocation to cheer a patient up,' Jack said wryly.

Kathleen heard the yell from her office, and shook her head. He was quite unmoved, totally untouched by the man's obviously severe injuries. It could so easily have been him—or her!

She felt sick again, and sat down with a plonk. Didn't he care about his life?

The answer was simple. No.

And why? Because there was nothing left any more for him to care about, and if his attitude over the past forty-eight hours was anything to go by, he was keeping it that way.

She wondered without any real hope whether he

would suggest they get together that night, and her level of optimism proved justified.

That he was regretting his impulse in inviting her to spend the weekend with him was obvious. What was equally obvious was that he had no intention of compouding his error with any further mistakes.

She went home — alone — and sat in darkness staring at the blank face of the television until eleven, and then she went to bed and stared at the ceiling instead.

CHAPTER SIX

TUESDAY was no better. Kathleen went out that evening and had a drink with a girlfriend, and got back to be told by one of her neighbours that the phone had been ringing.

Her heart leapt, but, rather than indulge her optimism, she rang her mother.

'Did you try me earlier?'

'I did. I've got good news — guess what?'

Kathleen sighed, ridiculously disappointed. 'Who's pregnant?'

'Patrick!' her mother announced with satisfaction. 'Well, not exactly Patrick, but Anne. The babe's due in January — isn't that wonderful? Of course, the cold weather's not ideal, but perhaps the next one will be a spring baby, and anyway the winters aren't so harsh these days what with heating and all — so, how are you, darling?'

'In love,' Kath told her glumly.

'Oh, darling, that's wonderful! Tell me *all* about him.'

So she did, sparing only the most intimate details.

'*How* old?' her mother asked, clearly appalled.

Kathleen sighed. 'Forty-one. Well, forty. Almost forty-one.'

'Oh. Well, if he's in good health I suppose that would be all right. After all, you're thirty now and no spring chicken yourself any more. So when are you bringing him home to meet us?'

'Mum, haven't you listened to a word I've said?' Kathleen yelled, and banged the phone down, tears of frustration in her eyes.

The doorbell rang, and scrubbing the tears off her cheeks with the back of her hand, she marched to the door and yanked it open.

'You!'

'I'm sorry—should I go away?' Jack asked a little too mildly.

'I wasn't expecting you,' she said ungraciously.

'I know—I tried to ring, but first you were out, then you were engaged.' He eyed her oddly. 'Are you OK?'

'No, I'm bloody well not!' she snapped.

She stalked away from the front door and it closed softly behind him. He followed her and cupped her slim shoulders in his big, comforting hands. Hah! I should be so lucky! she thought miserably.

'What's wrong, Irish?' His voice was soft, coaxing her. It did nothing for her temper. What's wrong, indeed.

'You are! You take me away for the weekend and then come back and act as if you've just met me at a friend's house for the first time! Damn it, Jack, after all we did——'

'I'm here aren't I?' he asked and his voice acquired an edge. 'I warned you not to take me for granted, Kathleen. I haven't got any ties, and that's the way I'm keeping it.'

She plonked on to the settee and it groaned in protest. 'I didn't think that meant you were going to pretend not to know me!'

'Oh, Kath——'

She snatched her hand away. 'Don't "Oh, Kath" me

in that tone of voice! What's the matter—getting cold at night again?'

'Would you like me to leave?' he asked quietly.

'No! Damn it, no, I want you to stay! I just don't see how you can kiss and cuddle me in the department when nothing at all is going on between us, and then just as soon as there is, you switch it all off like a blasted tap!'

He sighed and lowered himself to the other end of the settee. 'I thought that was what you wanted! You went nuts when Amy caught you sitting on my lap—'

'Are you thick? That was entirely different! Sure, I don't expect you to make love to me in the corridor, but even when we were alone you practically ignored me!'

He ran his hand wearily over his face. 'I'm sorry. I guess I'm not really used to this sort of thing any more.'

'What sort of thing—talking to a woman after you've spent a weekend in bed with her?'

'Yes,' he said frankly, and it took the wind out of her sails.

'What do you do?' she asked in horror. 'Just walk away?'

'Usually—on the rare occasions when I take a woman to bed. Sometimes there's a second or third date, but not often.'

She was appalled. 'Jack, that's awful,' she said shakily.

'No, it's safe. That way nobody gets to depend on me, nobody gets hurt. I never intended to have a relationship with you. If you hadn't come round that night, none of this would have been allowed to happen——'

'So it's my fault if I get hurt? Fine. Just so long as I know.'

'Kathleen, don't be sarcastic——'

'I think you'd better go,' she said unsteadily.

'Oh, Kath——'

'Don't touch me! This is hard enough.' She sniffed and looked up at him through tear-filled eyes. 'Why did you come round, anyway?

His face was etched with tiredness. 'I wanted to see you. I was fool enough to think you might want to see me.'

'Oh, Jack, of course I want to see you. . .'

He opened his arms and she flew into them, burying her face in his chest.

'Take me to bed,' she mumbled, and he laughed softly.

'I thought you'd never ask!'

'That's my line——'

'Shut up. Where's the bedroom?'

'Oh, I love it when you're masterful,' she teased, and got a glower for her pains.

'Where?'

'Left, at the end.'

'Right.'

'No, left.'

'Irish,' he warned softly.

With a giggle she slipped out of his arms and disappeared through the door, turning off the lights as she went.

'Come and get me!'

He growled, groped his way down the pitch dark corridor and found her almost by instinct. Her little shriek was cut off with unerring accuracy by the simple expedient of covering her mouth with his, and she gave up her struggles and surrendered, her foolish heart only too grateful for the crumbs he offered.

And if her head warned her that he only wanted her for sex, her heart ignored the warning and opened itself joyfully to his tender passion.

She was very careful after that not to take him for granted, even occasionally making excuses to refuse his sporadic invitations, although it tore her to shreds not to be with him at every opportunity. Just as she didn't take him for granted, she made sure he couldn't take her for granted either.

She even started making other arrangements so she wouldn't just end up sitting at home staring at the phone and forcing herself not to ring him and say her plans had changed and she was free after all.

She had dinner with Ben and Maggie Bradshaw, and Oliver and Bron Henderson had a party which she attended, although she ended up bumping into Jack as she might have known she would, and going home with him for the night.

Occasionally she went out for a drink with Mick O'Shea, who was between girlfriends at the time and was happy to have Kathleen along as pleasant and undemanding company. They had known each other for so many years, since they had trained at the Royal Victoria, Belfast, that there were no secrets or illusions between them and she was able to tell Mick all her problems.

Then one day another mutual friend from their days at the Royal Victoria breezed into town and ended up on Mick's floor for a couple of nights.

They arranged to go out for a drink on the second evening, although Kathleen wasn't really looking forward to it as it was bound to turn into a 'What was the name of that blonde with the big chest?' sort of session and she would end up driving them both home and quite likely putting them both to bed!

And then, at four-thirty when she was just contemplating going off shift, a call came in on the red phone that made her feel cold inside.

Jack was standing beside her at the time filling in notes, and she quickly jotted down the address and the scant details they offered, and turned to him.

'Toddler fallen out of an upstairs window and impaled himself on the railings. They want a flying squad.'

'Right. Ben!' he called, and Ben stuck his head out of a cubicle.

'We're off on a call—hold the fort, eh? Come on—we'll need to take some stuff—Haemacel, splints, airways, giving sets, saline—go and grab that lot while I find some coats for us.'

He ran down the corridor and Kath shot into the stores and grabbed the emergency bag and another unit of saline. He was back in seconds with Dayglo yellow coats.

'Here, put this on. We'll go on the bike—come on. Do you know how to find it?'

She glanced at the paper in her hand. 'Yes, I think so, but why don't we take my car?'

'No time, the bike's quicker. The traffic out there will be building up already, Kathleen. Come on, you'll be fine.'

'I will?' Blindly, she followed him, and in the entrance she bumped into Stan, a burly policeman in black waterproofs who was just heading out of the department. 'Stan, just the fellow. We have to go out on a call — kiddy stuck on some railings. Can you give us an escort?'

'Sure — where to?' He took the paper, nodded briefly and ran out to his bike, firing it up instantly. Jack chucked her her helmet, stowed the emergency gear and fired up his bike, and in seconds she was clinging on behind him as the sirens wailed and they took off through the car park as if the hounds of hell were after them. She was surprised to see that he had the green flashing lights of a doctor set into the fairing at the front of the bike, and a siren that almost deafened her. It was her last coherent thought for some minutes.

Stan was away, cleaving a path through the traffic so that all Jack had to do was follow him. Simple, except that Stan was probably doing almost sixty through the centre of town! Kath was terrified, but there was no way she was going to fall off unless she took Jack with her!

Finally they reached their destination, to find a huge crowd of silent onlookers all standing back a respectful distance and watching in mesmerised fascination as a distraught woman sobbed and screamed for help. She was kneeling on the steps next to the old iron railings that ran along the front of the terrace, her arms supporting the naked body of her little boy, and she was trembling with the effort of holding him still.

The crowd had parted to let them through, and Kathleen's fear for herself vanished as she took in the scene. The child had landed face down with his shoulders and arms across the railings, and the wickedly sharp spikes had pierced his tiny body in several places, mercifully passing each side of his neck. Incredibly, he was still alive.

Jack immediately commandeered two of the men to find a table and some pillows or something on which to rest the child's body, and with the help of a neighbour he managed to prise the terrified and exhausted mother away from her son.

Supporting his body with one hand, he quickly assessed him with the other. 'Right, he's still breathing. Let's get a line in fast,' he snapped.

It was already in her hand before he spoke, and by the time the men came back with the table and pillows they were running in normal saline through a line in his hand.

The ambulance arrived and the paramedics leapt out and ran up.

'How is he?'

'Still breathing — the spikes seem to have missed the main vessels in his neck, but the right brachial plexus may have copped it. Certainly his clavicle's gone. Possible head injury, maybe whiplash — he's unconscious at the moment. Hopefully he'll stay that way.'

Jack glanced up at Kath. 'Get an airway in, if you can. And we'll need pethidine drawn up in case he comes round — God knows how much. Work it out on his weight. I should say he's about twelve to fifteen kilos. He'll need a collar on just in case his neck's injured, but I don't know if you'll get it round the spikes. Where the hell are the fire brigade?'

'On their way.'

'Hmm. I hope they've got the sense to bring air powered cutters. I don't want him shaken to death, and we can't take him off these things. Can you get that airway in?'

Kath shook her head. 'No, he gags every time I try. I think he's hovering.'

Damn,' Jack muttered. 'I wanted him out of it. Give him the pethidine, then. Pity he didn't have clothes on, they would have cushioned his fall a bit. What the hell was he doing falling out of the window naked anyway?'

Stan, the policeman who had escorted them, had the answer to that. 'He was having a bath, and climbed to the end of the tub and fell through the window. The mother said she hardly took her eyes off him for a second.'

'Hmm. Well, you can't afford to at this age,' Jack grunted. 'Little kids are like quicksilver. How's the right radial pulse, Kath?'

She reached for the little wrist and laid her fingers against the inside. 'Very slight — less than the left, but it's still there. Perhaps the artery's just compressed.'

'Pigs might fly,' the paramedic muttered, and fastened the collar at last. 'Phew — let's hope that gives enough support.'

Jack ran a stethoscope over the boy's chest and pressed his lips together. 'Right lung's collapsed — he'll need a chest drain if he makes it. Oh, at bloody last — the cavalry. Let's hope they get him out fast, or we'll need an anaesthetist.'

The fire brigade van pulled up in a flurry of flashing lights and the crew were there immediately assessing the job.

'Soon have him free — take about half an hour to cut through that lot.'

'You can't have half an hour,' Jack argued. 'Get another set of cutting gear and tackle both sides at once.'

The man opened his mouth to comment, shrugged and went back to the cab. Minutes later another team appeared and they worked alongside. Even so, it was painfully slow and the little boy stirred and cried out in pain.

'Give him a little more pethidine, Kath,' Jack said quietly. 'Say two milligrams. I want to get his arm off this spike to save having to cut it as soon as they've finished the rest. He can't hang on any longer. I take it Theatre's ready for him?'

Kathleen nodded. 'Oliver Henderson's on standby and he'll have Andrew Barrett in with him.'

Jack nodded briefly and returned to his relentless checking of the boy's condition.

At last he was freed, and gritting his teeth, Jack took the small forearm firmly in his hands and lifted it quickly off the last spike.

The child screamed and sobbed, and Jack's face, usually so impassive, twisted with pain. He reached out and stroked the little head. 'Sorry, son,' he murmured, and then the crew lifted him off the table, pillows and all, and strapped him into the ambulance.

Kathleen went with them, Jack followed on his bike, and they raced back with sirens wailing.

The surgical team were scrubbed and in Theatre ready, but Andrew Barrett, the paediatrician, was waiting for them as they pulled up.

He walked swiftly beside the trolley as they wheeled it towards the Theatre lifts, and Kath told him as rapidly as she could what they had established.

'OK, he looks stable. Many thanks.'

Kath left them at the lift, and as the doors closed she caught a glimpse of him crouching down and talking to the little lad, his warm brown eyes kindly and concerned. She nodded. He was in good hands.

Jack was just arriving as she walked back into the department, and a police car drew up with the still-hysterical mother inside.

They led her into the interview-room, gave her a cup of tea and got her to sign the consent form—somewhat of a formality as the child was already in Theatre by this time, but at least that way they were covered in the event of any repercussions.

Then she and Jack placed the woman in the care of the duty staff and wandered down to the staff lounge to pour themselves the dregs of the coffee.

Jack flopped on to a chair and let his breath out on a sigh. 'Poor little bugger,' he said softly.

'He's alive—I reckon he'll make it.'

Jack dropped his head back against the chair and rolled it towards her. 'Yeah—maybe. God, those gawpers make me sick. Every time there's an accident, there they are, crawling out of the woodwork, eyes like saucers, lapping it all up. It makes me so angry—any one of them could have found something to rest that child on, but no, they all stand there in case they get blood on their hands and watch the child suffer—'

'Hey, Jack, it's just human nature.'

'Yes, well, there are times when I'm ashamed to be human if that's what it means.' He closed his eyes and dropped his head forward on his chest. 'I feel shattered—what time is it?'

'Nearly seven.'

'Fancy going to find something to eat?'

'That would be lovely. Do you want to nip home with me while I change?'

'Good idea.'

He unwound his long legs and stood up, arching his back and stretching. 'Come on, then, before I fall asleep.'

She drained her coffee, got her bag out of her locker and followed him out of the door. The traffic had almost disappeared and they arrived at her flat shortly after seven.

'What shall I wear?'

'Dunno — jeans? Nothing fancy. Come here.'

She went obediently into his arms and lifted her face to his.

'You did a wonderful job this afternoon,' he murmured between kisses, and she felt herself swell with pride.

'Thank you. You didn't do so badly yourself.'

He chuckled. 'You're too kind. Mmm. . .' His lips came down again and his hands slid down her back, urging her up against him. At once everything else receded, leaving them alone in a sea of passion.

His fingers dispensed with the buttons on the front of her dress and his hands, warm and firm and so, so clever, slipped inside and teased at the lace of her bra.

'Who needs food?' he mumbled against the lace, and his hot mouth closed enticingly over one nipple.

She sagged against him, her legs quivering, the blood pounding in her ears, and grabbed his shoulders for support.

Suddenly his head lifted.

'Don't stop!' she wailed, but he held her away from him, his face taut.

'Doorbell,' he muttered.

'What?'

The bell rang again, and this time she heard it.

'Who is it?' he asked.

She shook her head vaguely, still trapped in the magic of his kiss. 'I don't know. . .'

'Get rid of them.'

She nodded, and tugging her clothes back into some sort of order, she went to the door.

'Hi — you're not ready yet!'

'Mick!' She clapped her hand over her mouth. 'Oh, lord, I'd forgotten!'

He ran his eyes over her dishevelled clothing and smiled. 'So I see. Well, who's it to be? Your old friend, or your new lover?'

She closed her eyes. Oh, damn, she thought, how would she tell him?

Jack spared her the agony of making a decision by appearing behind her, helmet in hand.

'Don't let me spoil your plans — the lady's all yours, O'Shea.'

And with a brief, hard kiss on her lips and a curt nodd to Mick, he was gone.

It was a miserable evening. Her thoughts were definitely not with her companions, and after a while they dropped her back at her flat and went on to a club together.

She changed out of her glad rags, tugged on old jeans and a sweatshirt and drove out to his house.

The lights were all off, but that didn't worry her. She knew he often sat in the garden in the dark and listened to the sounds of the night.

She parked the car and looked around, but there was

no sign of him. His car was there, in the open barn, but the bike was missing.

She tried the back door and found it open, and going in she turned on some lights and made herself a cup of coffee. If the house wasn't locked, perhaps he'd gone to the pub to buy his horrible cigarettes or another bottle of Scotch to drown his sorrows — whatever, she didn't think he would have gone far.

She settled down to wait with a book on caving she found in his bookcase, but after a while she had to acknowledge he'd been gone longer than she'd expected.

Then she remembered he was on call, and used his phone to ring the hospital. Yes, he was in. There had been a gas explosion and there were several casualties. No, it was unlikely he'd be home for hours. No, she couldn't speak to him, he was with a patient.

She left his number with them and asked them to get him to ring, then made another drink.

When he called at a little before one in the morning, he was distinctly cool.

'What are you doing at my house?' he asked immediately.

'Looking for you — Mick and Terry have gone on to a club. You left in such a rush——'

He snorted. 'There didn't seem to be any point in a protracted farewell.'

'But, Jack, it wasn't like that——'

'Forget it, Kathleen. You're a free agent. How did you get in to the house?'

'Through the door, of course,' she told him crossly. 'It wasn't locked. I thought you were here at first, or just nipped to the pub or something.'

'Pub? It's one in the morning.'

'Yes, well, it wasn't then. Anyway, I soon realised you hadn't. What would you like me to do?' Wait for me, she wanted him to say, but of course he didn't.

'I've got my keys,' he said curtly. 'Just drop the catch on your way out. I won't be back before the morning.'

And he hung up.

Disheartened, she gathered her things together, locked the door behind her and drove home. Free agent, indeed! She was anything but, of course, but he wouldn't want to hear that. Oh, no. That implied commitment, and if you didn't have commitment, you could pretend you were free.

'Well, two can play at that game,' she said angrily. 'And anyway, who's taking whom for granted this time?'

Jack, too, was angry. Angry and frustrated and jealous as an ousted tom-cat.

OK, so her date with O'Shea hadn't turned out as he'd imagined, but the fact remained she had chosen her old college buddy over him — a fact that rankled for reasons he didn't care to examine.

Damn her! His body still throbbed in the aftermath of their interrupted lovemaking, and that too was irritating the hell out of him. He couldn't remember a time when going to bed with a woman hadn't dulled his interest, acting almost inevitably as a cure for his fascination.

But not with Kathleen. Oh, no, not with that aggravating, hot-tempered, sensuous little leprechaun. Far from slaking his thirst, all his weekend with her had done was whet his appetite and leave him with a desperate craving for more.

He had left her alone deliberately on that Sunday night, and again on the Monday, but by the end of Tuesday even his iron control had disintegrated in the face of his overwhelming need for her. Since then he had tried to stay away from her, and it seemed she was doing the same, which did nothing to cool his interest. Take tonight, for example — and just to turn the screw she had wound him to fever pitch before letting O'Shea in! Not that it had been difficult, he thought disgustedly. One touch and he was climbing walls for her.

An excess of teenage hormones, he told himself, lying desperately because the truth was too uncomfortable to face. He was still shocked that he had reacted so strongly when that jovial Irishman turned up. Damn it, O'Shea was lucky still to have all his teeth! Jack's fists clenched slowly until his knuckles stood out white against the tan.

She was getting to him, getting too close. What the hell was she doing at his house anyway?

He squashed the image of her curled up on a chair, feet tucked under her neat little bottom, waiting for him, her eyes drowsy and heavy-lidded —

'Damn!'

There was a knock on his door.

'Come in!'

It was one of the staff nurses. 'We could do with your help, sir, if you've got a minute.'

'Of course I've got a minute — what the bloody hell d'you think I'm doing here at this time of night?'

She blinked, apologised and quietly closed the door.

'Blast.' He looked down in surprise at his hands, and

consciously straightened them, flexing the fingers to ease the tension. Then he left the room and went to find the nurse who had been the unworthy recipient of his evil temper.

He growled an apology, gave the poor girl a miserable parody of a smile and turned his attention to their patient. Behind him he heard someone mumble something about pre-menstrual tension, and a wry chuckle escaped him.

There was a collective sigh of relief.

By the following day Kathleen's temper had cooled slightly, but so had Jack's attitude.

Back to that, she thought wearily. Oh, well.

They were as busy as ever, and her mood wasn't improved by the fact that she had to juggle staffing rotas and the pharmacy budget.

'I suggest we just let them suffer,' Ben said cheerfully. 'Who needs painkillers? Let 'em scream.'

'Ben, you're disgusting,' she said with a weary smile. 'How's Maggie.?'

'Throwing up. Pregnancy isn't suiting her. I think she's going to give up work soon so she can take it easy. She was giving up anyway when the baby came, so she might as well go a little early.'

Kath laid her pen down and leant back, smiling at him. 'Of course, with all that filthy lucre behind you you can afford to treat her like bone china.'

His mouth lifted in a wry smile. 'It has its uses.' He shifted awkwardly, then looked at her. 'How are you and the boss getting on?'

'Me and the boss?' she said innocently, struggling for air. 'OK. He's very competent.'

'Kath. . .'

Her composure crumpled. 'Ben, please, leave it,' she mumbled.

'Sorry — I didn't mean to pry.'

She gave a short laugh. 'There's nothing to pry into, Ben. We see each other every now and again, but we aren't joined at the hip like Siamese twins, you know.'

He chuckled. 'You ought to try it one day.'

She threw a paper cup at him. 'Go away and let me do my work, or we'll be running on one staff nurse and half an aspirin.'

And so she got through the week, surviving mainly on humour and philosophy, but occasionally resorting to sarcasm with particularly obtuse patients.

There was one woman who repeatedly used the unit as a GP's surgery. Kathleen had warned her countless times in the past, but this time she had had enough. The woman had a sore throat. Big deal, she thought, so have I.

'Is it very painful?' she asked briskly.

'Well, it is when I swallow or talk. I just need some antibiotics, really, I suppose, to clear it up.'

'How are your eyes?'

'My eyes? Fine.'

'Good. You see that sign up there? Could you read it to me?'

The woman glanced up at Kathleen, her face puzzled. 'Accident and Emergency.'

'Right. Which are you?'

'What?'

She took a deep breath. 'Have you had an accident?'

'Well, no, not really, it's just this awful pain in my throat.'

Kathleen was feeling the pain a lot further down, in the region of her tailbone.

'Is it an emergency?'

'Well, I — I suppose it needs treating fairly quickly.'

'Mrs Forbes, there are people in here who have got broken bones, or severe chest pain from heart trouble, or head injuries, or crushed limbs from industrial accidents. There are people who have been brought in unconscious for no apparent reason, who have had car accidents and been cut free by the fire brigade and rushed in for *emergency* treatment following *accidents*. None of them has a sore throat. Do you understand?'

'Well, yes, it could be a great deal worse ——'

'And it would have to be before you require our services. Now perhaps you would like to go to your GP in the normal way and get him to deal with your throat.'

'But he's always so busy ——'

'Mrs Forbes, we are busy. The average waiting time in here is nearly an hour. How long is it at your general practice?'

'Oh, at least half an hour ——'

'So you could have saved yourself half an hour by going there.'

'But he always seems so tired and stressed.'

Kathleen could have screamed.

'Mrs Forbes, I am tired and stressed. My staff are tired and stressed. The medical profession as a whole is tired and stressed, and frankly, people like you don't help!'

'Well, there's no need to be rude!' the woman snapped, and snatching up her bag, she stalked off.

'Well, that was tactful,' Ben said from behind her.

'What's happened to our warm and sunny Sister Hennessy?'

'I'm tired and stressed, didn't you hear?'

Ben smiled sympathetically. 'You and me both. Let's go and have a cup of coffee and deal with this lot later. Judging by the look of them they aren't much worse than her. I tell you what, why don't you throw them all out and we'll have the day off?'

'Don't tempt me,' she said with a wry laugh, and picked up the next file. 'Hold the coffee. We'll get this lot moving and then stop. Mr Grieves, please? Could you come with me?'

By Friday she was unable to be philosophical any longer. She was lonely, and she wanted to see him. She wasn't alone. Several times she caught him looking at her unguardedly, and heat flared in his eyes, to be instantly banked as he brought it under control with his iron will.

But it was enough. She knew he wanted her, and even though it was only for her body Kath was so desperate for his attention that she was ready to settle even for that.

She hated herself for it, her pride and her need constantly at war, but finally by lunchtime her need won. She found him in his office. 'Jack?'

He stiffened at the soft sound of her voice, and his head lifted, his eyes carfully veiled.

'Yes, Kathleen. What can I do for you?'

I thought we were lovers! she wanted to scream, but she swallowed her hurt for the thousandth time and forced a smile.

'Are you busy tomorrow night? I thought I'd cook us a meal at my place. . .'

He stood up and paced to the window, his back to her. 'I won't be here. I'm off to Yorkshire tonight and I won't be back until Sunday afternoon.'

'Sunday, then,' she said, and damned herself for the note of desperation in her voice.

'I'll be late — God knows what time it'll be.'

'Well, why don't we leave it open? If you're back in time, come round,' she suggested, and hated herself for grovelling.

'OK, but don't bother to cook for me. I'll grab something somewhere.'

Well, she wasn't about to push her pride any further for him. She lifted her chin.

'Fine. Have a good weekend.'

'Thank you. You, too.'

Fat chance, she thought dismally, the prospect of two days and three nights without seeing him yawning ahead of her like the Grand Canyon. She left his office quietly, too raw to make a scene and attract attention, wanting only to crawl into a corner and hide.

The weekend was every bit as long and lonely as she had anticipated. The weather forecast on Sunday was for rain, and she thought of him riding his bike back down the motorway in poor conditions and had to revive her anger to stop from worrying herself sick over him. Instead she attacked her flat, scouring it within an inch of its life, and finally collapsed exhausted into the bath at five.

Not really hungry, she made a cheese sandwich and curled up in front of the television. She was just in time for the tail end of the early evening news, and her attention was immediately caught.

' . . .go back to Tim Styles at Ingleborough,

Yorkshire. Tim, I gather you've got some news on the three missing pot-holers?'

Kath's heart slammed against her ribs, and she felt the blood drain from her face.

'Oh, no, it can't be him—he can't be there still. . .'

The picture cut from the newsreader in the studio to the rain-lashed Yorkshire countryside and a reporter standing huddled against the driving rain.

'In the last few minutes one of the party of missing students——' Kath let out her breath on a gust '—has made his way to the surface, and he has told us that there are still two men trapped below here,' he announced in the earnest voice of sepulchral doom so favoured by reporters at the scene of an incident. 'One man has apparently sustained a serious head injury after the belay on his rope failed and he fell fifty feet down a pitch to the rock floor.One of his companions has remained with him; a third, the one who sounded the alarm, is returning to the scene of the accident with the rescue team, which you can see gathering behind me.

'Conditions are not on their side. The rain which is making conditions up here decidedly unpleasant is as I speak seeping through the rocks and creating foaming torrents underground, flooding caverns and making passages impassable. There is one ray of hope—one member of the rescue team, himself an experienced caver, is a Casualty consultant from Suffolk who has volunteered to go down with the party to provide immediate medical assistance to the injured man. He's here with me now. Dr Lawrence, is there anything you can add?'

CHAPTER SEVEN

THE camera cut to Jack, fully equipped in Neoprene suit and helmet. Kath's heart stopped, and then started again with an untidy lurch. What was he doing there? He should be on his way home! He couldn't go down — didn't he know it was dangerous?

Then he was talking, explained what they hoped to do. 'The most important thing is to get medical aid to the injured man as quickly as possible. As with any sort of head injury, time is of the essence. It hasn't been raining very long, and the quicker we can move, the more likely we are to get them out before conditions deteriorate to the extent that the passages become impassable.'

'Is that likely? Do you know the area where the men are?'

Jack nodded. 'Yes, it's a pot I've been down many times — not the easiest; apart from a fifty-foot pitch we'll have to haul him up, there's a long sump we'll have to bring the injured man back through which could be tricky if he's unconscious or uncooperative. Also the main passage is a minor water course, but in rain like this it tends to swell. The more it rains, the fuller the stream will get and the bigger the problem, so really, time is the most important factor, especially as we don't really know what we're going to find when we get down there.'

134

'Can you give us any idea how long the rescue will take?'

He shook his head. 'Some time. It'll take us a couple of hours to reach them, and at least twice as long on the return, plus whatever time we have to spend getting the patient stable enough to move. As I said, the sooner we start, the sooner we'll have them out. In fact, if you'll excuse me, I believe we're ready now, so I must go.'

The reporter thanked him, and the camera tracked him as he trudged over to the other members of the team and they headed together towards a dark crack in the hillside. Then the camera returned to the reporter, who promised to keep the viewers updated.

The newscaster then switched to a trivial item about a cat who'd been rescued from the roof of the houses of Parliament, and Kathleen flicked off the set and threw her sandwich in the bin, her appetite gone.

What if he died? What if the rain increased and they were trapped underground by a flood that washed them away down one of those awful little squeezes? They would be lost forever, their bodies never recovered. . .

She clamped her hand over her mouth and caught the sob, then forced herself to breathe nice and steadily, in, out, in, out — she wouldn't panic. She wouldn't!

The phone rang, and she snatched it up.

'Hello?'

'Kathleen, it's Mick.'

She knew from his voice that he had seen the news too, and she had never been so glad to hear a friendly voice. 'Mick! What am I going to do?' she wailed. She could feel the panic rising again, but she was helpless to control it.

'Stay there, I'll come round. Put the kettle on.'

She did as she was told, moving mechanically, conscious of her heart flailing erratically against her ribs.

Mick came and made some tea and sat her down with a cup in her hands and tried to talk some sense into her.

'He knows what he's doing. He isn't going to take foolish risks.'

'Mick, going down there is a foolish risk — didn't you hear what he said?'

'I heard — and you know you'd go yourself if someone needed you.'

'Humph.'

'Humph yourself. He'll be fine. Drink your tea.'

'It's disgusting, you put sugar in it.'

'You need the sugar, you're shocked.'

'Rubbish, I'm just. . .'

He caught the tea before it toppled, and sat and held her while she howled her eyes out.

Finally she straightened up and glared at him balefully. 'That was all your fault. You shouldn't have been so nice to me. Now your sweatshirt's all soggy.'

'Hmm. I'll probably get rheumatism in my shoulder and nobody to blame but myself. That'll teach me to make tea for unstable women——'

He ducked the cushion and handed her back her cup. 'Finish this, love, and we'll wander down to the pub while it's not raining.'

She shook her head, feeling the dread clutch at her again. 'I don't want to leave the flat. There might be some news——'

'There'll be nothing for hours. Come on, a quick drink in your local.'

He was right, of course, she knew that, but she picked up the brandy Mick got her and downed it in one, then hovered on the edge of her seat until he gave up and walked her home.

They spent the evening with one eye on the television, playing cards and drinking too much coffee. There was a newsflash at nine to say that the rescue party had reached the injured man and were now returning to the surface, and then nothing until almost midnight.

Then, suddenly, the programme was interrupted by a newsreader who announced that the party had just reached the surface. They switched live to the scene, and Kathleen's eyes immediately picked out Jack crouched over the injured man and issuing instructions to the ambulance team. As soon as the ambulance pulled away the reporter made his way over to Jack.

'This is Dr Lawrence, who led the rescue. Dr Lawrence, what can you tell us about the condition of the injured man?' he asked him.

Jack looked up and wiped a grubby hand wearily over his face, streaking the dirt still further. His smile was wry.

'Much as I would love to claim all the credit, I must point out that my part in this rescue was very small indeed. The Yorkshire Cave Rescue Organisation is a very skilfully orchestrated operation, and they all know exactly what they're doing. Most of the time I was simply in the way. As for the patient, it's not my place to comment on his medical condition, except to say that he is still quite definitely alive and in the best possible hands.'

'What will happen to him now?'

'He'll be transferred to hospital for a whole series of tests and X-rays, and the results will determine the treatment he's given. He's had a very long and trying ordeal, and apart from his physical injuries he's had the cold and damp to deal with too, so his body's had a pretty severe challenge. Other than that, I'm afraid I can't comment.'

'Is he conscious?'

'I'm sorry, I can't comment on that.'

'The rescue took less time than you anticipated. Is that because the conditions underground were better than you'd expected?'

Jack shook his head and gave a wry laugh. 'No, rather the reverse. It was very wet, getting worse, and I didn't feel that the patient could tolerate sitting out flood waters, so we moved as fast as we could.'

'What about getting him through the sump? Let me explain for the benefit of viewers that a sump is like a U-bend in plumbing, permanently full of water, so that the only way through is to dive under the water. That must have been very tricky with a seriously injured patient.'

Jack gave a weary chuckle. 'Let's just say that the CRO have done that sort of thing before and it was all over very quickly! Now, if you'll excuse me, I could do with a bath and something to eat.'

The reporter signed off, and Kathleen stared at the screen as Jack's image was replaced by the film that had been running. She hadn't realised how tense she was until she heard that he was all right, but now she crumpled like a wet paper bag, laughing and crying and laughing again all at once, while Mick hugged her and passed her tissues.

He opened a bottle of wine he found in one of her kitchen cupboards, and they celebrated Jack's safety to the sound of Kathleen's tearful giggles.

'Are you OK now?' he asked after a while, and she nodded.

'Oh, yes. I was just so worried. . . I'm fine. You go on home. Thank you, Mick, you've been wonderful.'

He hugged her hard. 'You're welcome. I wish I had someone who cared as much about me.'

'Oh, Mick, there'll be someone. And if she's lucky, you'll love her, too.' She turned away, unable to talk any more, and felt Mick's warm hands pull her back against his chest.

'Oh, Kathleen, how could he not love you? Just give him time.'

She sniffed and pulled away. 'Mmm. Anyway, you'd better go, it's late. Will you be all right driving after that wine?'

He shook his head. 'Not really. I'll walk home and pick the car up in the morning.' He dropped a quick kiss on her cheek and let himself out, and she wandered round the flat, tidying up the bits and pieces and generally winding down.

Then, with nothing else left to do, she crawled into bed and slept fitfully, her mind filled with images of Jack's beloved, dirt-streaked face laughing into the camera.

She was woken at half-past five and listened for the sound that had disturbed her. A motorbike? Not Jack's. He would have rested up there for the night, of course, and would drive down in the morning. With a sigh, she snuggled down under the quilt again.

*   *   *

The bike was in his space when she got to work at eight. Stunned, she did a mild double take and almost ran into the department.

'Morning, Sister!' the nurses chorused.

She smiled vaguely at them and made her way to Jack's office. He was on the phone, and after glancing up briefly at her, he ignored her until he'd finished.

'You should be resting,' she told him then.

'I'm fine,' he said shortly.

'No, you're not, you're exhausted, and you aren't fit to work at the moment. Why don't you take the duty room and go and lie down for a couple of hours?'

He drew in a deep breath, paused for a second and let it out on a sigh. 'You're right. OK. But wake me at eleven, or sooner if you need me. Understand?'

He was cold and remote, shutting himself off from her completely. Pain, sharp and unexpected, swamped her.

'Yes, sir. I understand,' she said quietly.

She walked away, her head held high, and fought down the tears. Why do I care about you, you bastard? she thought miserably. God knows you don't deserve it! I don't know why I waste my time.

She took the report, went out into the department and threw herself into her work with tight-lipped determination.

Those who had seen her in this mood before faded quietly out of reach; others got their fingers burnt.

Amy Winship and Joe Reynolds, predictably, were among the others.

Amy failed to monitor someone's blood-pressure adequately and it was only because Kathleen bothered to check that a potentially life-threatening internal haemorrhage was detected in time.

As for Joe, who blithely missed a fracture a yard across, she could have pinned him to the wall with a scalpel, she was so cross.

'Take a sight test,' she advised tightly, and he flushed and apologised, which just made her more angry.

At quarter to eleven her old friend Jerry, the Valium addict, wandered in complaining of stomach pains and said he'd taken another overdose.

'Oh, Jerry, not today,' she groaned.

He peered at her owlishly, his eyes strangely sympathetic. 'No?'

'No—not unless it's for real.'

He nodded and walked away, and Kathleen closed her eyes.

'Jerry?'

He stopped.

'Come on, let's check you over anyway.'

She found a staff nurse to help her and they washed him out, finding nothing as she had expected, but she sent a sample of the stomach contents off for analysis anyway.

Then she took Jack in a cup of coffee.

He was lying on his back with the sheet round his waist, one arm flung up over his head, and she could see bruises all down the underside of his arm and down his ribs.

She set the coffee down on the little table and perched on the edge of the bed.

'Jack?'

He stirred and opened his eyes.

'Irish. . .what's the problem?'

'Nothing. It's eleven. I've brought you a cup of coffee.'

His eyes drifted shut. 'Thanks. Just leave it there, I'll get it in a second.'

His deep, even breathing told her he had fallen asleep again, so she slipped out of the room and left him to it.

Ben was in the staff-room. 'Jack OK?'

She nodded. 'I think so. He's covered in bruises all down his ribs — God alone knows what it was like down there. I've left him sleeping. What's afoot?'

'About twelve inches.'

She summoned a wry smile, and he relented. 'Nothing much. Joe's reducing a dislocated thumb if he can screw up the courage, and Amy's changing a dressing. I'm not sure I can bear to watch.'

She tutted. 'Amy's fine now. I've gone through her sterile trolley techniques until she can do them in her sleep, likewise all the other nurses.'

Ben snorted. 'She still manages to stick her fingers in the swabs with monotonous regularity, then she says 'Ooops!', grins and chucks them out and opens another pack.'

'At least she realises she's done it now.'

Ben rolled his eyes. 'That's better?'

The phone rang, and Kath picked it up. 'Sister Hennessy.'

It was ambulance control. They had been called out to a little boy who had been playing behind the family car when his father had reversed it out of the garage. He had apparently sustained leg and head injuries, and was coming in, complete with hysterical parents.

'I gather they're in a hell of a state, so be prepared,' she was told.

She cradled the receiver. 'On your pins, Bradshaw, and you'd better get your wife down here.' She outlined the case briefly, and Ben winced.

'Aah! Don't know if Maggie can cope with that, she was a bit rough this morning. I'll see if Peter Travers or Andrew Barrett are around. We'll also need orthopaedics and neurology, and possibly a surgeon. Shall I wake the boss?'

Kathleen shook her head. 'No, let him sleep for now. We can always get him if we need him.'

They heard the siren and were at the entrance ready to take over as soon as the boy was carried out of the ambulance.

True to the controller's word, the parents were beside themselves, the mother sobbing and screaming accusations, the father grim-lipped and shaken, white as a sheet and obviously badly shocked.

She detailed Amy to take them into the interview room and give them tea and stay with them, and she and Ben went alongside the trolley into Resus.

The child, a boy of about two and a half, was unconscious and bleeding from a gash on his head. While Kathleen wired him up to a monitor and put in an intravenous line, Ben ran gentle fingers over the boy.

'Nasty head. Probably hit it when he fell. Abdomen seems OK. The right leg seems to be the worst — looks as if he was crouching and got knocked sideways by the bumper, then run over,' Ben said briskly. 'His foot's crushed, and the tib and fib are both broken. Heel too,

I think. There's no degloving, anyway, thank goodness.'

Kathleen was just releasing the cuff. 'Normal — touch low, as you'd expect.'

Kath looked up and saw the paediatrician approaching. 'Morning, Andrew.'

'Morning. Oh, dear, poor little tyke. Where are the parents? I'd like some history.'

'Knocking hell out of each other in the interview-room, I think. I sent a junior nurse in there with them to referee, but I expect by now they've got her pinned to the wall,' Kath told him.

Andrew's brows twitched together. 'Who did it, then?'

'Father. Usual story — reversed out of the garage, didn't look behind, child playing on the drive.'

'Oh, God, why don't people learn from other people's mistakes?' the big man muttered, and bent over the child. 'May I?'

'Be my guest,' Ben said, and stood back out of the way while Andrew examined him gently but thoroughly.

'Seems fit enough — don't like the look of that head injury.' He traced the gash with a fingertip. 'Nasty bump — I think we need to look more closely at that. How are his pupils?'

'Still reacting, but a little uneven. I've ordered an EEG,' Kath told him, and he nodded.

'OK. Let's see what that turns up. I think we'll put him in special care when he comes out of Theatre.'

'Tim Mayhew's coming down to look at his foot. I gather Barrington's in Theatre already,' Ben added.

'Fine. Well, I'll go and see the parents. They're making enough noise to wake him up.'

Just then the noise increased dramatically, and was suddenly cut off again by a slamming door.

Amy appeared in tears.

'Problems?' Kathleen asked her.

'I tried to help,' she said, valiantly suppressing her tears. 'They didn't seem to want to know.'

'May I ask the thrust of the argument?' Andrew Barrett asked. 'It might save me from being shoved through the door like you.'

Amy ran a tearful eye over his not inconsiderable bulk and smiled damply. 'I'd like to see them try it!' She tipped back her head and took a deep breath. 'Mum says he should have looked first, Dad says if she'd been keeping an eye on him he would have been fine. Mum says he should have shut the door when he went back into the garage and he wouldn't have been followed. Dad says he did shut the door——'

'And Mum doesn't believe him. Typical. Don't worry, thanks for trying. I'll go and talk to them.'

'She also said if he'd gone like he said he was going to, this would never have happened and they would all have been a lot better off.'

Andrew made an O with his lips and nodded. 'Thanks.'

He left the room just as Jack appeared, his hair rumpled, his shirt half-tucked into his trousers, tie hanging round his neck. He glared at Kathleen.

'What the bloody hell's going on? It sounds like World War Three.'

'I should say that about sums it up,' she said drily, and turned her attention back to her patient, leaving explanations to the others. Hurt by his icy reception this morning, she was quite happy to avoid him.

She managed it until lunchtime, when he came into the staff room just as she was leaving.

'Any coffee left?'

'I expect so,' she said, and went to move past him. In doing so she jarred his arm, and he flinched slightly.

She gave him a narrow look. 'Are you all right? Do you want someone to look at you?'

'I'm fine, they're just bruises and the odd dent.'

'Did something go wrong?'

He laughed shortly. 'Let's just say I got in a tight spot.'

She looked away. 'I saw you on the television.'

He sighed. 'So did half the hospital, I gather.'

'I didn't expect you back until later.'

His mouth compressed into a hard line. 'No, I gathered that, too.'

She was puzzled. He had been so angry all day, but why? 'I don't understand. What do you mean? Am I supposed to have done something wrong?'

He let his breath out on a harsh sigh. 'Oh, come on, Kathleen, cut the crap. I saw O'Shea's car outside your flat this morning.'

She met his eyes, startled. 'It *was* you, at half-past five. I woke up, but I told myself it couldn't be you because you'd be in Yorkshire —'

'How convenient — was he there all weekend?'

She stared at him, stunned. 'You think — Jack, for God's sake! Mick's an old friend —'

'An old friend, or an old lover? Or don't you bother with the distinction?'

Anger took over from shock. 'Well, damn you, Jack

Lawrence, how dare you talk to me like that? He may not be as stinking, filthy rich as you, but he's worth ten of you any day of the week! At least he knows how to treat a woman!'

And with that she stalked off, head held high, and it was only later when she calmed down that she realised he still thought Mick had stayed the night.

'Well, tough,' she muttered. 'Let him think what he likes. Arrogant pig.'

Their contact after that was brief, professional and kept to the absolute minimum. It was impossible to avoid each other in such a hectic department, but fortunately the very business of it meant that any and every contact was necessarily fairly brisk.

And that suited Kathleen fine.

Her anger kept her going for the best part of two days, but then Mick bumped into her and asked how Jack was, and she told him, in words of one syllable.

'He thinks you stayed the night.'

Mick sighed. 'Damn, if only I hadn't had that wine and walked home — well, the man's a fool. Tell him that if there'd been any chemistry between us at all, I would have married you years ago and if he had any bloody sense he'd do it now — in fact, forget it, I'll tell him myself.'

Kathleen panicked. 'Don't you dare do any such thing, Mick O'Shea! You leave well alone, you've done enough damage. Anyway, it makes a useful armour.'

'Armour?' Mick was furious. 'Damn it, Kathleen, don't you go using me as a shield. If you want out of that relationship, you tell him. Don't hide behind me to do it.'

She sighed heavily. 'I don't want out of the relationship, Mick. It's just that sometimes — well, I don't even know if we have a relationship, and I don't want him thinking he can take me for granted.'

Mick shook his head slowly. 'You're trying to make him jealous? Forget it, he isn't that kind of man. If he can't have you all to himself, he won't want you at all. He's not a man who'll share his woman, and I don't blame him. I wouldn't be in a hurry to share you, either.'

'Huh. I don't frankly think he cares enough either way to worry. He was just annoyed because he came round and thought you were there.'

'At five-thirty in the morning? You're not telling me he'd ridden all the way from Yorkshire after the gruelling day he'd had, just to enjoy the pleasures of your delightful little body! Even Superman needs his sleep, Kathleen.'

She flushed and lifted her shoulders in a little shrug. 'God knows what he wanted. He isn't about to tell me now, anyway. Look, I'm going for lunch. You keep your nose out, you hear me? One word to him and I'll have you in a pot roast.'

Mick grinned. 'You and whose army?'

Kathleen shook her head and turned away, walking down the corridor towards the canteen. She didn't see Jack appear at the end of the corridor behind her, or see Mick lift his head and meet the level gaze.

Nor did she see Mick walk towards Jack, or see the expression in his eyes.

If she had, she would have turned straight round and come back, but she didn't, she kept on walking.

*　*　*

'I want a word with you, O'Shea,' Jack growled.

The man smiled lazily. 'Well, isn't that just a nice little coincidence?'

Jack opened his door and ushered Mick in with exaggerated courtesy. He wanted a cigarette. Damn it, his hands were shaking, but he had to know.

'I'm not sleeping with her,' O'Shea said quietly, 'nor have I ever done. There was a time I might have tried, back eight years or so, but there was never any chemistry. If there had've been, we'd be married now, because I love her, but not like that — not the way you love her.'

Jack's head snapped up. 'I don't love her.'

Mick's smile was slow and gentle. 'So why do you care that I was with her that night?'

Jack turned away and pulled a cigarette from his pocket, fumbling with his lighter. Damn the man, what was he saying? Was he with her or not?

'Were you?' His voice sounded like handfuls of gravel were stuck in his throat.

'I had been, earlier. I saw the news and went round to keep her company while she waited.' He paused, unsure how much to say. 'Oh, what the devil,' he said softly. 'She was in a hell of a state, Jack. She was so scared for you, and when she saw that you were OK, she just fell apart. I talked to her, we had some wine, and I walked home.'

Jack dropped into his chair and let out his breath on a ragged sigh. 'Oh, God. I thought — I knew she'd be worried, but I didn't want to ring. For some reason I thought it would be better just to go to her so she could see I was all right.'

He paused, struggling for words. 'I know she loves

me — at least, I thought she did, and then I saw your car. . . She said you were worth ten of me.'

He forced himself to meet Mick's eyes.

'I can't give her what she wants from me, Mick. I wish to God I could. . .'

Mick laughed softly. 'She wants any damn thing you're prepared to give her, and that's a crying shame, because she deserves a hell of a lot more than that.'

Jack stood abruptly and turned to the window. Damn, why was everything out of focus?

'I know she does,' he said, and his voice was ragged. 'I thought if I stayed away from her. . .but I can't. I need her, but I can't love her — '

'You do love her.'

'No!' He shook his head, and repeated, softly, 'No. No, I mustn't. There's so much I can't give her — so much she deserves, so much she ought to have. I thought — perhaps if you two were — maybe she'd be OK with you.' He ran a hand through his hair, unable to deal with the sudden wave of emotion the conversation had brought with it. He took a steadying breath and turned back to face Mick, ticking off points on his fingers.

'Look, I'm divorced. She's Catholic. She'll be under pressure to get married, and there's no way I'm going to get married again, ever. I can't give her children, and she'd be a wonderful mother.'

'She doesn't want children, Jack.'

'She says.'

Mick sighed. 'She's a grown woman, I think she knows what she's talking about.'

'Maybe.' The phone rang quietly, and he picked it

up. 'Lawrence. OK, I'll be down.' He cradled the receiver. 'Sorry, I have to go. Look, Mick. . .'

Mick held out his hand. 'Forget it.'

Jack grasped the hand and shook it firmly. 'Thank you for being there for her.'

'Don't thank me, just get round there and talk to the woman.'

He made a non-committal noise, and Mick grinned.

'In your own time, of course.'

Jack returned the grin wryly. 'Of course.'

'Why do people always ring the doorbell when I'm in the bath?' Kathleen grumbled, and climbed out of the tub, grabbed a towel and ran down the hall. 'I'm coming, hang on — Jack!'

Flustered, she clutched the towel closer and gazed wide-eyed round the edge of the door.

'May I come in?'

'I was in the bath — give me a minute.' She shut the door in his face, too hurt and confused to allow him in until she was safely dressed.

She tugged on her jeans over damp legs, cursing and falling over on to the bed, struggling with the clinging fabric until she had them hitched finally over her hips. Then she grabbed a sweatshirt and tugged it over her damp hair, not bothering with a bra.

Refusing to allow herself the indulgence of looking in the mirror and repairing her make-up, she walked slowly back down the hall and opened the door again with trembling hands.

He was slouched against the wall, his helmet under one arm, and he shrugged slowly upright, his face impassive.

'May I come in now?'

'That depends what you want.'

'To talk to you.'

She turned away. 'Is there anything to say?'

He followed her in. She heard the door shut softly behind him, then the dull thunk of his helmet on the hall floor.

'Mick came to see me.'

She whirled round, her eyes flashing. 'Damn him! I'll kill him. I told him —— '

'Irish, please let me talk.'

She looked up at him, and for the first time she saw emotion in his eyes.

'Sit down,' she said shakily, and took the chair. That way she could watch him, read his face, find out perhaps what he really meant. . .

He lowered himself on to the sofa and unzipped the top of his leather suit. She noticed his fingers were trembling, and her anger faded, replaced instead by a wild and optimistic hope.

'I was coming to see you,' he began, and his voice was low. 'I knew you'd have seen the news, and I wanted you to know I was OK. I knew you wouldn't be expecting me, but I really — I needed to see you, too,' he confessed, 'just to be sure I was still alive.'

She knew he was talking about the rescue now. So many times she had helped at the scene of an accident and felt the same need to be with people afterwards, just to be sure, as he said, that she was still alive.

'Was it really grim? You looked exhausted.'

He nodded. 'It was hell down there. There's a watercourse that runs along the bottom of the passage, and you have to make your way along above this slit

with water pouring through it. Usually it isn't too bad,
but on Sunday the water was lapping at our ankles, and
if you slipped you could feel the current tugging at you.
If he hadn't been so badly injured we wouldn't have
even attempted a rescue until later, but he was in a bad
way, so we had no choice.'

'How bad was he?'

Jack shrugged. 'How bad can you get? Depressed
skull fracture, uneven pupils, ragged reflexes — and
more fractures than I care to think about. God knows
how he was still alive. The water was rising all the
time, and we had to seal him inside a waterproof bag
and drag him through the sump.' He paused, his eyes
firmly fixed on his hands.

'He got stuck — the stretcher caught on a rock. I was
with him, holding the drip inside the bag, and I had to
wrench him free and get out before we ran out of air.
That was grim. Then one of the team slipped in the
passage and went under the water. We were all roped
together, so we got him out, but it was a close thing.
He could easily have got a foot stuck and he would
have drowned. That was when I realised how much
you mattered to me.'

He looked up and met her startled eyes. 'I think I
love you, Irish,' he said softly, and his voice was gritty
with emotion. 'It doesn't change anything. I'll never
get married again, so don't hang around waiting for it,
and don't expect to have me at your beck and call,
because that isn't how I am. But I do want to see you
when I am around, and be with you.'

'When you haven't got anything better to do, you
mean?' she said sadly.

'No, Kathleen.' He stood up and began to pace, like

a restless lion. 'That isn't what I mean at all. I can't let you take over my life. I have to be independent. I can't allow myself to rely on anyone, and I can't cope with anyone relying on me. That has to be fundamental to our relationship, but it doesn't mean I don't care.'

Their eyes locked, and slowly she rose to her feet. God help her, she was doing something very foolish, but she couldn't walk away.

She held out her hand, and after a second he took it. Wordlessly, she led him to her bedroom and turned towards him, reaching for the long zip on his leather suit.

'Kathleen——'

She placed a finger on his lips. 'Don't talk. Just let me love you.'

She dragged the zip all the way down and eased the top over his shoulders, leaving his arms trapped behind him while she ran her hands lovingly over his chest. He was wearing a T-shirt, and she slid her hands beneath it and threaded her fingers through the soft curls on his chest.

She felt the groan against her palm, and smiled impishly, raking her nails slowly over his ribs.

His body shuddered, and then his tolerance disintegrated and he wrenched his arms free and wrapped them round her, holding her hard against him.

'Don't tease me, Irish,' he whispered, and his voice was a ragged thread.

She eased away from him and unzipped his boots, tugging them off before sliding the leathers down over his long legs. His T-shirt followed, and his briefs, then she pushed him towards the bed and stripped off her jeans and sweatshirt.

'Aren't you lying down yet?' she chided gently.

He reached for her, and then they were falling to the bed in a tangle of limbs and caresses and fevered kisses.

Their loving was wild and tempestuous, with no time to spare for tenderness or softly spoken promises. He was demanding, but so was she, both of them raging out of control, riding the wild storm that flung them helpless before it, clinging to each other as the only certain thing in a world gone mad.

Then he stiffened, harsh shudders racking his body, his head flung back as if in agony.

'I love you!' he gritted, over and over, the words torn from him, and Kathleen felt the world splinter all around her.

'Oh, Jack, I love you, too,' she whispered, and his arms tightened round her, holding her hard against his heaving chest, and she turned her face into his shoulder and wept.

CHAPTER EIGHT

THEY lay in the half-dark, lit only by the street lamps that shone through her open curtains, their legs tangled together, fingers linked on top of the quilt.

Kathleen was curled on her side watching him as he drew deeply on his cigarette.

'You ought to give that up,' she chided gently.

He grinned. 'Confucius he say the three best things in life are a drink before and a cigarette after.'

She giggled. 'I bet he never said such rubbish.'

'He should have done, then.' He stubbed it out and turned towards her. 'I got rough again; I'm sorry.'

Her lips curved slightly. 'Don't apologise, it was wonderful.'

He looked away quickly. 'Irish, don't look at me like that.'

'Like what?'

'With those great big eyes with love written in them in letters ten feet high.'

She pulled away, hurt. 'You can't make love to me like that and then expect me to carry on as if nothing's happened. I'm not one of your sophisticated women, Jack. You know I love you. I can't hide it and I won't. I'm sorry if it makes you uncomfortable.'

He rolled on to his back, one arm behind his head, staring rigidly at the ceiling.

'There's so much I can't give you. Marriage, chil-dren — so much you ought to have. Every time you

156

look at me like that it just reminds me that I'm cheating you, short-changing you. I wish I could be what you want, but I can't. I'm sorry.'

'But, Jack, you are what I want——'

'No—no, I'm not, and I never will be.'

In the dim orange glow from the street lights, she saw a solitary tear trickle down his cheek and run into his hair.

'Jack?'

He turned to her blindly, his lips searching for hers and then clinging as their bodies met and meshed, their movements gentle now, their loving a balm to ease the sadness in their hearts. And when it was over and their tears had dried, they lay like spoons, curved together as if made for each other, and slept.

Kathleen had told Jack she couldn't hide her love. Over the next few days she was to find out just how true that was.

'Eh-up, Cupid's been at it again,' Ben Bradshaw said in a lousy Yorkshire accent.

'Well, Sister Hennessy, at last you fall victim to the mystery virus,' Jesus Marumba murmured with a wicked twinkle.

Only Mick said nothing, preferring for the good of his health to keep out of her way.

Of course, it wasn't made any easier by the fact that Jack was attracting a great deal of interest, anyway.

Andrew Barrett, the paediatrician, came down to the department on the Thursday morning to deal with an admission, and grinned at Jack. 'So, how's the big TV star today, eh?'

'Oh, for God's sake,' Jack said with an embarrassed laugh.

'Leave him be, Andrew, he makes a lousy hero. Coffee?'

'Thanks.' He settled into a chair with a big sigh and took a sip, then blinked. 'Gosh, this is better.'

Kath rolled her eyes. 'Not you too! How's the boy who was run over?'

He grinned. 'Driving us nuts. His foot's still elevated, so he can't fidget about, and that's tough on a little boy. No after-effects from that nasty bump on the head, though, and the parents have finally stopped fighting and started pulling together.'

'Oh, well, they say every cloud has a silver lining. How's the little chap on the railings?'

'Jeremy? He's fine. Going home tomorrow. He had a narrow squeak, that one.'

'Any permanent damage?' Jack asked.

'Don't think so. Possible slight nerve damage to the right arm—the brachial plexus was a bit chewed up, but he's been remarkably lucky. Bit concussed, of course, following the whiplash. He must have stopped falling pretty abruptly. Otherwise he was fine. Broken humerus and clavicle, again on the right. He'll need a bit of physio to sort that out when the cast comes off, but the chest drain was out after a couple of days, and his lung's working well.'

'Lucky.'

Andrew snorted. 'I'll say. That's another parent with problems, of course. The mother's on a bit of a guilt trip.'

'Of course,' Kathleen agreed. 'I don't know how these women cope. It would drive me crazy.'

Andrew smiled. 'Oh, I don't know. I love kids. Well, obviously, or I wouldn't be a paediatrician, but I'd be quite happy to have dozens.'

'How many have you got?' Jack asked.

'Of mine? None that I'm aware of,' he said with a grin. 'I'm not married. Never found anyone mug enough to have me. How about you? How many have you got?'

'Me?' Jack looked away, and then looked back. 'None — now. I lost my son three years ago to cystic fibrosis.'

Andrew's compassionate brown eyes registered shock, and then regret. 'Ah, hell, I'm sorry, I had no idea — forgive me for asking.'

Jack waved his hand. 'Forget it. Not talking about it doesn't make it go away.'

'Nevertheless, I trampled on a nerve. I apologise.' Andrew set his cup down and unravelled his long legs. 'Back to the grind. Thanks for the coffee, Kathleen.'

Kathleen watched him go. 'He's a nice man. Very quiet, but super with the kids. They all love him. It's a shame he's not married, he'd be a wonderful father.'

'What about you?' Jack said softly. 'You'd be a wonderful mother, but you aren't married either.'

'Well, for the first, as far as I'm concerned they don't go without the second, and for the second, I don't believe I'm about to be asked.'

She met his eyes steadily, and after a moment he turned away with a sigh.

'No — I'm sorry, Irish.'

She walked away, her heart heavy. Nothing had changed, except she could now admit to her love. The only difference was that they now spent some of their free time together, thus giving her even more opportunities to fall more and more deeply in love with him.

And she did, of course, despite all warnings to herself. He was away that weekend hang-glinding, and asked her to go with him. She refused, because as she said she had no urge to sit on a draughty hillside and watch him break his miserable neck.

In the event it was too windy to fly on the Sunday so he came back early and they spent the day in his garden preparing an area of lawn for seeding.

It was almost, she thought heavily, like being married, except that they weren't and never would be. His absence the previous day had brought that home as nothing else had. In a vain attempt to maintain her independence, she spent Monday and Tuesday nights at home — alone. It didn't work.

On Wednesday he came and found her just as she was finishing off applying a back-slab to a fractured wrist. After the patient had gone, he hitched one hip up on the couch and watched her clear up.

'Time on your hands?'

He smiled. 'Not really, I was just enjoying the view. I've missed you. Actually, I wanted to ask if anyone had said anything about HIV testing after our messy suicide.'

'Nothing to me, and I'm sure I would have heard. Ben certainly isn't worried, and I know I'm not, and Amy took herself out of range pretty swiftly.'

He chuckled. 'Wise, under the circumstances. Are you done? There's a woman waiting with a query fractured toe.'

He slid off the couch, wincing as he put weight on his foot.

'Is your ankle playing up again?' she asked sharply.

'Yes — and don't say a word!'

'Who, me? Would I? Where's this fracture, then?'

The woman had, indeed, broken her big toe. The fracture was clearly visible on the X-ray, and even Joe Reynolds could have seen it.

'My daughter told me she'd spilt nail varnish on my new bedroom carpet.'

'You shouldn't have kicked her so hard,' Jack said with a grin.

She laughed. 'Wretched child. I fell up the stairs running in my socks to clear it up. I'd just come in from the garden and kicked my wellies off when it happened.'

'How did you get here?' Kathleen asked her.

'My husband came home from work. Do you know what he said? Not "Poor thing, I'll be right home," but "Did you have your shoes on?" Self-righteous pig!'

Her husband laughed. 'Well, you never have shoes on. I've always said you'd hurt yourself one day. Perhaps now you'll listen to me.'

'You see?' she said, and rolled her eyes. 'Virtue personified.'

'Well, he can atone for his sins by waiting on you for a few days,' Jack said laughingly. 'I'm afraid it's going to be a bit sore, but as it's such an impressive break we'll put a garter strapping on to help immobilise it. Come back in a fortnight and we'll check its progress, but you'll find it takes a few weeks to really heal properly because we use that toe a great deal for balance.'

He left Kathleen to strap the toes together with a gauze swab between them to maintain the alignment, and then sent them off with a few coproxamol for the pain.

'Only eight?' Jack asked as they went.

'Think of my pharmacy budget,' she told him.

'The reality of medicine,' he said drily.

Their next patient, however, demonstrated the unreality of medicine. He was fitting, very convincingly, on the floor of the waiting area when she went back, and Joe Reynolds was hovering over him.

'Oh, not again!' Kathleen groaned.

'What?'

'Leave him to get on with it. He's a faker.'

Jack watched him for a moment, impressed, then winked at her and strolled off, whistling.

Joe was less convinced. 'Are you sure?' he asked anxiously.

'As the sun will rise in the east. Name's Harry Parker, a.k.a. John Hendy, Simon Smith and Peter Blake. He's an old friend. OK, Harry, up you get before you hurt yourself.'

The man hesitated, then clamped his teeth in a rictus and twitched off again.

'Harry! You're making a mess on my floor. Now get up, stop showing off and go home, please!'

The convulsions subsided and he seemed to go into a coma. Joe still looked worried. 'Sister, don't you think we ought to do an EEG? He's not responding to pain stimulus.'

She nodded. 'He's good. It's no good pinching his ear, you have to do something more dramatic, like kick him in the crutch.'

Harry curled up tighter and groaned, then opened his eyes. 'Where am I?'

Kathleen gave a humourless little laugh. 'Harry, we're busy. We don't have time to play games. Now get up, sit over there and you can have a cup of tea before you go home.'

He shambled to his feet and glared at her balefully.

'It worked last time. I got a bed for the night.'

'Are you back on the street?' she asked, immediately concerned.

'They threw me out of the hostel. I missed a night — well, I felt claustrophobic. Think I'll go back to London, more hospitals there. Got more chance of fooling them.'

She laughed. 'Why don't you try RADA? You've got a great acting career ahead of you if you could only learn a few more tricks.'

Joe looked slightly shocked. After settling Harry down with a cup of tea, she led Joe into her office and sat him down.

'Why would he want to do that?' he asked, clearly puzzled.

'Attention, a bed for the night as he said, something to do — he's a bright guy, but he lacks intellectual challenge. Fooling us gives him a buzz.'

'Well, he certainly had me fooled.'

She resisted the urge to say that wasn't difficult, and sent the poor boy off for lunch.

She went into Jack's office to find him on the phone.

He winked and waved her to a chair, then turned his attention back to the caller. After few moments he hung up.

'Humph.'

'What, humph?'

'Friend — chap at the Beeb. Wants us to do a part-recorded, part-live "Day in the Life of Accident and Emergency" thing.'

'What? Why us?'

Jack shrugged. 'Old Pals Act. He saw me on the television the other weekend. They had a hospital all lined up, and they've had to cancel because of staffing problems. I said I'd discuss it with you.'

'Oh, God — when?' Kath was totally bemused.

'Friday week.'

'Fri — oh, no. Not a Friday night! Are you nuts? All the drunks and the brawlers and the RTAs — are you crazy, Jack?'

'I haven't said yes yet.'

'Yet.'

'Yet.'

'Well, don't bother. They'll cause havoc.'

He leant back in his chair and grinned. 'Might be rather fun. They're very good, you know. They've done this sort of programme before, quite often. They won't get in the way.'

'No, well, they'd better not. I'm not having anyone underfoot. They get between me and my patients, at any time, for so much as a nanosecond, and they're out, I don't care what it does to their scheduling.'

Jack grinned. 'I'll pass all that on, shall I?'

'You do that!'

'I suppose you *are* on duty?'

'You bet your sweet life I'm on duty. No way half the BBC is coming into my department without my supervision!'

'I'll ring him back and say yes, then.'

She straightened. 'I never said that.'

That wicked smile played around his lips. 'No? Quote, "No way half the BBC is coming into my department without my supervision," unquote.'

'Damn you, you're a manipulator, do you know that?'

He chuckled and picked up the phone. 'Better book yourself a haircut, Irish—oh, and have it dyed red to go with the temper. They're more likely to take you seriously then.'

She picked up a Biro off his desk and levelled it at him. 'They'll take me seriously, just you watch them!' She laid the pen down. 'I'll go and check the rota. Joe Reynolds and Amy Winship might just find themselves with a long weekend!'

She left the room to the sound of his deep chuckle.

The programme dominated the next week and half, to the exclusion of almost everything else including common sense. They had endless meetings with the producer and the reporters who would be covering the day, and Kathleen laid the law down with such charm and skill they almost didn't notice.

But, as Jack had said, they were professionals, used to working alongside other professionals without impeding their progress, and familiar with the intricacies of confidentiality and patient etiquette.

'No filming anyone who doesn't want to be filmed, and any flicker of sensationalism and you'll be out,' she told them on Thursday night, her smile for once absent.

They nodded agreement. 'We don't need to sensationalise,' the producer told her wryly. 'Usually we have to back off and tone down, because although the public have an insatiable appetite for gore, the camera crews get a bit queasy.'

She chuckled. 'Is that a fact? Well, Friday nights round here there's plenty to make you feel like that!'

Their meeting finished, the last details all sewn up, the crew headed for the door.

As they were leaving the producer paused and smiled at her. 'Don't worry, Sister Hennessy. We won't get in your way. The crew know what they're doing.'

She returned his smile slowly. 'Fine — just so long as they understand that I mean what I say.'

Jack looped an arm round her shoulders and tugged her up against his side. 'Don't worry, Bob, I'll lock her in her office if she becomes a nuisance.'

She laughed and punched him none too gently in the side. 'Nuisance yourself,' she scolded. 'You behave or *you'll* be locked up. Too much exposure to the camera already, that's your trouble. Think you're a celebrity or something.'

'Quite right, too.' He turned his head. 'Which is my best side, Bob?'

'The one without the black eye,' Kathleen said drily, and the team wandered off, still chuckling.

'Early start tomorrow,' Jack said. 'I'd better go back to my place — my suit's there.'

'Suit?' Kathleen did a mild double take. 'Did you say suit?'

He shrugged. 'Thought I ought to present the right image —— '

'Oh, my God. . .' She rolled her eyes. 'Will we know you?'

He refused to rise to the bait, instead giving her a quick kiss on the lips and heading for his car. 'I'll see you in the morning — bright and early.'

She grinned. 'You bet — I have to get this place kicked into shape by eight.'

She ironed her dress carefully when she got home, and in the morning she climbed blearily out of bed at six to wash and dry her hair. Still she was in the department before seven to find the camera crew busy setting up unobtrusive lights in strategic places, and the cleaning staff putting the finishing touches to the floor.

She was accosted by a make-up girl who fluffed about with powder and asked her about eye make-up.

'I don't wear a great deal for work,' she explained, 'and I have no intention of going on air looking like a tart, so forget it.'

'Perhaps a little subtle shading?' she suggested diplomatically, and Kathleen surrendered.

'OK, but be quick, I've got a lot to do.'

'How's that?' the girl asked, but then the phone rang and there was no time to worry because they were swinging into action with the RTA, two victims of a car smash who came on a blue light with sirens wailing.

Kathleen and Jack ran to meet the ambulance, Kathleen taking over the bagging of one of the victims who had arrested in the ambulance.

They rushed him through to Resus, and got him going again, and while Kathleen put the monitor leads on Jack checked him for injuries and ordered X-rays.

It was only some time later when he was safely on his way to Theatre that they realised the whole lot had been filmed.

'Excellent,' Bob said enthusiastically, 'brilliant start to the day.'

Kath blinked. 'I wonder if our patient would agree

with you,' she said drily. 'I hope someone's at home videoing it for him.'

'Roll up, roll up for the Greatest Show on Earth,' Jack cried expansively, waving his arms around.

Kath flicked her eyes over his soft cotton shirt and cord jeans. 'What happened to the suit?'

He wrinkled his nose. 'I thought better of it. Not me, is it, really?'

She laughed and shook her head. 'Not really, but you might do up your top button and shove your tie up a bit — my mother's watching this.'

He rolled his eyes. 'Mine, too. I shall have such a lot to answer for.'

The day performed beautifully for them, right through to the evening, and then things started to go wrong.

They lost a patient, a young woman in her twenties who had thrown herself out of a car at speed to get away from her husband. It was messy and tragic and Kathleen wanted to cry for her, but the cameras kept rolling and she shrugged it off and carried on.

Later she caught up with Bob, the producer. 'That young woman — was that on live, or can we cut it?'

'No, it wasn't live — why do you want to cut it?'

'I just do,' she said stubbornly, and he agreed.

'OK. It's your department.'

'Thank you.'

She walked away, confident that the whole messy incident would be forgotten, but she was wrong.

True, they didn't show the filming of their frantic attempts to resuscitate the desperately injured girl, but they did show Kathleen emerging from Resus., tears in her eyes, telling the cameraman to get out of her way, and then they showed a brief interview with Jack where they discussed the case in scant outline, and also her reaction to the death.

'We tend to think we can do anything,' he said wryly, 'but we can't. We can only resuscitate, we can't resurrect. And yes, it hurts. You get mad, sometimes you cry, then you pick up the pieces and get on, because there's always someone else who needs you.'

She went and found Bob.

'You told me you were going to cut that.'

'We did.'

'No, you didn't. OK, you didn't show the gore, but you didn't cut it right out, either.'

He tried to reason with her. 'Kathleen, it was important —'

'What, to see me cry?'

'Yes.'

She glared at him, then sagged. 'I'm sorry. You're probably right. It won't do the public any harm to think we care about them, but I'm not used to being watched.'

'You're doing fine,' he assured her, and with a curt nod she went back to her work.

Amy Winship, severely threatened, was on duty and came to find her. 'Sister, that guy who threw up on you is here — says he wants to see you.'

'Oh, hell — where is he?'

'Cubicle Two.'

'Come with me,' she sighed, and twitched the curtain aside. A cameraman appeared at her shoulder. 'Not this one,' she said firmly, and he grinned and walked away.

She turned back to the man slumped in a chair in the

cubicle. 'Right, Jerry, what the hell are you up to, tonight of all nights?'

He gulped and shook his head slightly. 'Nobody will listen. It's just too much. Always, the craving—please, Sister. You've got to listen to me. I can't go on.'

'Have you taken anything?'

He shook his head.

'Look, Jerry, we're rushed off our feet. Come and see me on Monday, and we'll get you an appointment with a psychiatrist, OK?'

'It's too long.'

'Well, it'll just have to be. Now come on, we need this room.'

She watched him shuffle away, her heart troubled. Had she done the right thing?

'He looks really sad,' Amy said. 'As if, this time, it really is too much.'

Kath nodded. 'Watch him, Amy. Follow him, if you have to. I don't think he'll go far. Just keep an eye on him, talk to him if you want. But whatever you do, don't give him so much as a cough sweet!'

She went on to the next cubicle, a simple fractured thumb that even Joe Reynolds had managed to diagnose and set without too much trouble.

She passed Jack in the corridor and he winked at her. 'How're you doing?'

'OK. I had a go at Bob.'

Jack grinned. 'He told me. Listen, I want to grab some supper. Coming up?'

'What, and leave Amy and Joe without either of us riding shotgun?'

He chuckled. 'They'll survive.'

'Yes, but will their patients? Anyway, Amy's out

watching Jerry to make sure he doesn't do anything daft.'

'Jerry?'

'Carrots in the frilly—remember?'

The grin widened. 'Oh, *that* Jerry.'

'The very same. I just have a bad feeling about him.'

'Look, I'll go and get a couple of sandwiches and bring them back down. If you've got a minute you could fill up the coffee machine again, and I'll have a word with Jerry when I get back down.'

'OK.'

Just as she was turned away Ben called her. 'Got a kiddy with a nasty scald—can you give me a hand? We need some pethidine, I think, or even diamorph.'

She ducked into the cubicle, hardly conscious of the cameraman tucked into the corner. The child, a girl of about five, was whimpering softly, the skin of her legs and bottom already peeling.

The mother was distracted almost out of her mind. 'She must have decided to run herself a bath—I can't believe it. The water really isn't that hot, usually, but my other one was fiddling with the boiler earlier—he must have turned up the thermostat. Oh, God, will she be all right? I put her in cold water till the ambulance came, but I didn't know what else to do!'

Kathleen squeezed her hands quickly. 'That was fine. We'll get rid of the pain with some drugs, and then transfer her to the burns unit at Cambridge. She'll be OK. Don't worry.'

Ben glanced up from the child. 'Flamazine, Kathleen, I think, and paraffin gauze to protect her skin, then I think we need to get her moving. We'll give her diamorph, and we need saline to boost her fluids.'

He asked the mother the child's weight, worked out the dose and Kathleen went to draw up the drug and get the Flamazine ointment. Jack went past Resus and hailed her, and she popped out into the corridor. 'Can you check this with me?'

'Sure. I've got your sandwich. Everything OK?'

'Uh-huh. Just stick it on my desk, I'll have it later. Oh, could you ring Cambridge? Child for the burns unit — Ben's got the details, Cubicle Four.'

'OK.'

She double-locked the drugs cupboard and went back to Ben. 'Here we go.'

Very soon the child was calmer and they were able to cover the damaged skin and prepare her for transfer.

Sue, one of the reporters, followed them to the door and then turned to Kathleen. 'So, what will happen to her now?'

'Now? They'll clean her up, get lots of fluids into her because the main danger is dehydration, and then she may need skin grafts to repair some of the areas. Depends on the depth of the burns. Until a specialist has seen her, I wouldn't like to comment. Excuse me, I think I'm needed.'

Amy was hovering out of camera range, looking decidedly worried.

'What is it?' Kath asked her quietly.

'Jerry — he went into the men's a few minutes ago and he hasn't come out.'

'Oh, lord — I'll get Jack to check. Well done.'

She found him in her office eating sandwiches and downing the last of his coffee.

'Would you like to go to the loo?'

He blinked. 'Pardon?'

'Jerry. Just go and check on him. He's up by the entrance and I can hardly go in there, can I?'

Jack sighed and swung his legs off the desk. 'Eat your sandwich while you've got ten seconds. I'll be right back.'

She picked up the sandwich and took a bite, and then heard Jack's yell.

She ran up the corridor to the gents' loos and barged open the door. 'Jack?'

'In here — he's slashed his wrists. Get me some rubber straps, fast.'

'Here.' She tugged two strips of rubber tube out of her pocket. 'Never leave home without one,' she said with a grim laugh, and helped him drag the unconscious man on to the floor. 'Oh, help, there's blood everywhere — we need to get him in Resus. quick. Hang on.'

She stuck her head round the door and spotted a porter. 'Alvin? Get a trolley in here, quick. Amy, come and help.'

She saw a cameraman hovering, and glared at him. 'There's no room — unless you can fly?'

They hauled Jerry on to the trolley and ran down the corridor to Resus., the cameraman in hot pursuit. Sue was talking as they went, describing the scene, and Kathleen realised they were on air live again.

Still, there was no time to worry. They sat him up, hauled off his jacket and shoved up his sleeves, reapplying the tourniquets as quickly as possible.

'Get a line in, Kathleen. We need two units of Haemacel PDQ — Amy, jump.'

'PDQ?' she asked, clearly puzzled.

'Pretty damn quick,' Kathleen and Jack said in unison, and exchanged a grin.

'Oh — right.' Amy disappeared, and Jack shook his head.

Seconds later she was back, the Haemacel in one hand, a small white container in the other. 'I found this on the floor — I wondered if it might have fallen out of his pocket.'

Jack took it from her and turned it over in his hand. 'Ibuprofen. It's empty.'

'Would they do him any harm?'

'A hundred? Oh, yes — massive gastric bleed. Oh, damn. OK, Kathleen, let's pump him out.'

They connected up the drip, set it running and turned him on to his side. Amy, by now familiar with the routine, fetched a bucket and a sterile lavage tube from CSSD, and Kathleen ripped open the packet, lubricated it and passed it down his throat with ruthless efficiency.

'Coffee gounds — damn, he's bleeding. OK, we'll flush him and put him on forced diuresis. He'll need a catheter. We'd better get Marumba down here.'

While Jack and Kathleen dealt with the patient, Amy rang the switchboard and asked them to pass the message on to Dr Marumba.

Minutes later he turned up, briskly efficient, and ran his eye over the patient and the charts.

'Pressure's very low. We'd better have him in ITU I think.'

Jack nodded, his head bent over the worst of the wrists, suturing the ugly slash. 'I'm only doing the blood vessels; the tendons need a surgeon if he gets that far.'

'OK, we'll just dress it. What about the other one?'

'Just a dressing, I think. Perhaps butterfly sutures. This was the really clever one—probably the first. I don't suppose he had the strength in this hand to do the other very well.' He sat up and stretched, then stripped off his gloves. 'OK, take him away, that's all we can do.'

'Do we have notes on him?'

Kathleen rolled her eyes and slapped a dressing on his wrist. 'Half a rain forest,' she said drily. 'He's an old, old friend. Just take him away while you still can. I'll contact ITU and get a porter. Coffee?'

'No, I haven't got time. Later, perhaps.'

She phoned ITU, and then told Jesus that they were ready for his patient. 'Alvin, could you take Jerry down to ITU?'

Then she turned back to the reporter. 'Gory enough for you?'

Sue grinned weakly. 'Well done. I don't know how you cope.'

Kathleen gave a hollow laugh. 'Nor do I sometimes. I'll just have a mosey round front-of-house and see what's going on,' she told Jack.

He nodded. 'Try to find time for your sandwich, too.'

'Will do. See you in a minute.' She turned to Amy, who was clearing up the dressing trolley. 'Well spotted, Amy. If you hadn't found the bottle, he could well have died.'

She coloured, and her jaw sagged slightly before she recovered. 'Thank you, Sister,' she mumbled, and turned away, grinning like an idiot.

Oh, well, I've made somebody's day,' she said to

herself as she walked briskly through the department, running her eye over the smooth operation of the unit.

Technically speaking, of course, she was off duty now and one of the night sisters had responsibility for the unit, but there was no way she was handing over until the camera crew went home.

Jack was on call anyway and had more reason to be there than her, but if anything that was an added incentive to stay.

There was a brawl going on in the entrance, and two policemen were clamping handcuffs on a couple of young men who were causing the trouble. A third, clutching a filthy rag to his face, was threatening them with all manner of retribution.

'You'd better watch your mouth, mate, or we'll have you, too,' one of the policemen advised him.

Kathleen felt a prickle between her shoulderblades and knew the camera was approaching. So, too, did the two boys in handcuffs, who immediately started swearing violently and accusing the police of unnecessary brutality.

Kath shook her head. 'Get them out, Stan, we don't need them in here. You, come with me. It's your turn to be a star.'

She towed the grumbling adolescent down the corridor and into a treatment cubicle. 'Right, sit down. Name?' She took his details, cleaned his face up and put a few butterfly plasters over the cut. 'It'll heal cleanly, so you won't have a scar to ruin your beauty. It was a nice, sharp blade evidently.'

'Glass — bastard bottled me.'

'You want to press charges?'

'Wot? 'E's me bruvver.'

'Charming family,' she muttered, and sent him on his way.

She turned to the camera and grinned. 'The things people do for entertainment round here on a Friday night!'

The cameraman winked at her, and she shook her head laughingly and went back out to Reception. There was no time for her sandwich, so she worked her way steadily through the next three cases.

She was just finishing with the last when there was a shout from Reception.

She ran round there and found a woman collapsed on the floor, blood oozing from a cut on her arm and another on her thigh. Her face was bruised and battered, one eye swelling rapidly, and she was mouthing, 'Help me, please help me,' over and over again.

Kathleen grabbed Amy and they lifted her on to a trolley and wheeled her into Resus.

The cameraman followed, but apart from telling him to keep her face out of shot Kathleen ignored him.

'Don't let him in here—keep him away from me,' the woman whimpered.

'Don't worry, pet, you're OK. We'll look after you. He won't get you here. What's your name?'

'Tracey—Tracey Ford. He isn't my husband. I live with him. There's the kids, too—I want them got away from him. I wouldn't have left them, but I thought he was going to kill me.'

'Go and find Ben or Jack, could you, Amy? And if the police are anywhere about, get one of them in here, too. Otherwise call them.'

She had the woman stripped and covered with a

blanket in moments, and bit her lip to contain her anger.

'How long's this been going on?' she asked gently as she cleaned up a nasty cut on the woman's arm.

Her face screwed up in a mixture of pain and self-disgust. 'Years,' she confessed. 'Years and years. He always promises, and then he's fine till next time — ow!'

'Sorry.'

Just then there was a crash and a roar from reception, and Tracey seemed to shrink with fear. 'That's him — oh, God, no, please!'

'Where is she, the whore? I'll kill her this time, she's gone too far, telling everyone. Where are you, bitch? Lying cow, I'll find you. . .'

The door crashed back and Kath turned to see a huge man, dressed in a pair of filthy jeans and a tatty old string vest and carpet slippers, swaying in the doorway and brandishing a lethal-looking kitchen knife.

Tracey screamed, and he lurched forwards.

'Oh, no, you don't!' Kath vowed, and, snatching up a stitch-cutter, she held it in front of her. 'You lay a finger on her and I'll kill you myself. Put the knife down.'

'Bloody IRA trash — get out of my way!' he roared, and lunged at her.

CHAPTER NINE

JACK was in the staff-room watching the programme live with Bob when he heard the racket in Reception.

Seconds later, the television showed a drunken gorilla brandishing a knife at Kathleen—his Kath!

'Bastard, I'll kill him!' Jack muttered, and tore down the corridor to Resuscitation, sending a dressings trolley flying.

He could see Kathleen in front of the treatment table, clutching a stitch-cutter like a lifeline, and as the man lunged at her he threw himself forward and grappled with him, falling with him to the floor.

Despite his drunkenness the man was still immensely strong, and there was a nasty moment when Jack could feel him gathering his strength, but then suddenly there was a dull thud and he went limp.

'Jack?'

Her voice was tentative, shaken, and he got slowly to his feet, searching her face.

'Are you OK?' he asked.

'Of course—are you all right?'

'Of course? What do you mean, of course? Damn it, he nearly killed you!'

'Well, he won't do any more damage for a while. I've knocked him out.'

Jack closed his eyes and sagged against the wall.

'Do you have any idea what I felt like when I saw you facing up to him with that silly little blade in your hand? Do you have any *conception* of what it felt like to know I was about to lose you?'

'Do I——?' Kathleen put her hands on her hips and squared up to him. 'Well, Holy Mary, Mother of God, you've finally seen the light! Do *you* have any idea how I've felt, weekend after weekend, knowing you're crawling down muddy holes or chucking yourself off cliffs? Not to mention every day of the week when you climb on that evil machine and ride off into the sunset!'

'That's different——'

'How is it different? It doesn't feel any damn different from where I'm standing!'

'You aren't fit to be allowed out,' he growled.

'Yeah, well, you and me both, then.'

'I mean it! You need a keeper——'

'Huh,' she snorted. 'Over my dead body!'

'Yes, well, you nearly managed that just now!'

'I did not!'

'You did—look at you! For God's sake, woman, he could have killed you!'

'So what's it to you? I thought I was a free agent?' she spat at him.

'Damn that,' he growled. 'I'm going to marry you and lock you up out of harm's way.'

'Oh, are you, indeed?' Her eyes flashed sparks. 'And with whose permission?'

'Yours, dammit.'

'You haven't asked me yet.'

'Well, I'm asking you now,' he roared. 'Marry me!'

'OK.'

'What?'

'But there are certain conditions.'

'Conditions?' His eyes narrowed. 'What conditions?'

Kathleen was enjoying his downfall, he could see that. She lifted her hand and ticked off on her fingers. 'One: you stop pot-holing. Two: you stop hang-gliding. Three: you sell the bike. Four: you give up smoking.'

He gave a short laugh. 'Anything else?'

'That'll do for now.'

'And what do I get in return?'

She grinned impishly. 'Me, in your bed every night.'

A slow smile spread over his face. 'Done.'

'You're a pushover, do you know that?' Her face crumpled slightly. 'Could I have a hug, please?'

He stepped over the recumbent body on the floor and swept her up into his arms, crushing her against his chest as his lips came down hard on hers.

Then, slightly bemused, he lifted his head and stared round at the cheering crowd that had gathered in the doorway. 'Oh,God,' he groaned, and rested his head against hers. 'I think I just proposed to you in front of most of Great Britain.'

She giggled. 'Good. You won't be able to wriggle out of it, then. Too many witnesses.'

'But you may want to.'

'No way.'

He kissed her again, lightly this time, conscious of the crowd and the cold dread that was touching him. There was something he had to do, and he didn't know if he could find the courage. 'We'll talk later.'

He straightened away from her and turned his attention to the man on the floor. 'I hope he's not been brain-damaged by that blow.'

On the treatment couch, Tracey snorted. 'If he is, they'll never tell the difference. Are you two really OK?'

Kathleen laughed and hugged her gently. 'Never better. I've been trying to pin him down for weeks.'

Jack grunted, conscious only of the icy fear that gripped him.

Suddenly the room seemed too crowded, and he stood up and glared at them all. 'Haven't any of you got any work to do?' he snapped. The crowd faded, and he turned his attention back to the unconscious man at his feet.

It took four of them to lift him on to a trolley and take him away for observation, with the police riding shotgun at his side, and then things gradually returned to normal—or as normal as they could given the extraordinary circumstances.

Kathleen was called to the phone and discovered her mother crying and laughing all at once, with all the family, it seemed, lined up behind her waiting to talk.

'I'll speak to you later. Of course I'm all right. All in a day's work. No, Mum, you can't talk to Jack, he's busy. I'll speak to Patrick tomorrow—no, Mum, I can't. Goodbye.'

She put the phone down and looked up at Jack.

'Busy, am I?' he said quizzically.

'Mmm—kissing me.'

'Uh-uh.' He backed off, the dread clutching him again. 'I'm through kissing you in public. Let's put this film crew to bed and then go home.'

She grinned. 'Sounds good to me.'

His heart wrenched.

It was some time before they were able to leave the hospital, and they went straight to Jack's barn. Despite the lateness of the hour, the phone was ringing when they got in.

'Ah—hi, Mum,' Jack said, and rolled his eyes at Kath. She smiled and went and put the kettle on, and listened as he wriggled like a worm on a hook. Finally she went and took the phone out of his hand.

'Mrs Lawrence? It's Kathleen. Don't worry, I won't let him get away. I'll be sure and get him to call you tomorrow. Goodnight.'

She grinned at him. 'See? Easy.'

He passed her the phone. 'So ring your mother.'

'No way! I'm avoiding her. Why do you think I'm here?'

'You're here,' he said softly, 'because we have to talk.' He set the phone down with exaggerated care. 'Nothing's changed, Irish.'

'Yes, it has,' she answered just as softly. 'We've both realised what we mean to each other. When I saw you struggling there on the floor with that evil man, I realised there was nothing I wouldn't do for you, or you for me. That's when I realised that I couldn't go on with this free agent nonsense. I need you, Jack, just as you need me. Without you, I'm empty.'

'Oh, Irish. . .'

He held out his arms and she flew into them, wrapping her arms tight round him and hugging him hard.

'Take me to bed, Jack.'

He fought it for a second, then gave in. 'My pleasure,' he murmured, and, lifting her easily into his arms, he carried her up the stairs and lowered her into the middle of the huge old bed.

He undressed her slowly, his eyes travelling over her skin as he revealed it, making it flush.

'You're so lovely,' he said huskily, and her throat had a great lump in it suddenly that threatened to choke her.

She reached for him, and he stripped off his clothes and lay beside her, taking her tenderly in his arms.

Suddenly he started to shake, his whole body trembling in reaction.

'I thought I was going to lose you,' he grated. 'I thought that bastard was going to run you through with that knife and take you away from me——' His voice broke and he dragged her closer, burying his face in her hair. 'Don't ever do anything like that again— promise me.'

'I promise. I just didn't think. He was going to kill her, and I was just—there, I suppose. Jack?'

'Mmm?'

'Make love to me, please?'

His hand reached up and brushed the hair back from her face, and then he was kissing her, his lips warm and gentle. She felt as if he was paying homage to their love, his every caress a thanksgiving, and for once the wildness left them alone so their loving was a thing of tenderness and healing, of joy and celebration.

Afterwards he held her gently and smoothed the tears from her cheeks, heedless of his own.

His sigh was heavy, though, and she felt it all the way through to her bones.

'What's wrong, darling?' she asked him softly, her hand over his heart.

'Oh, Kath, there's so much I can't give you. You deserve more,' he said heavily. 'Much, much more.

Things haven't really changed, you know. I still can't give you children — well, only if we use IVF and they screen the embryos — always assuming my vasectomy could be reversed.'

She shook her head. 'I couldn't do that, Jack. I think *in vitro* fertilisation is wonderful for childless couples, but I could never consider that option for us. Perhaps I'm more of a Catholic than I thought, but the idea of all those discarded embryos — it makes me feel cold inside.'

His fingers threaded through hers and curled over his heart. 'But it's the only way I'd consider. Even if you don't carry the gene, one of our children or grandchildren or great-grandchildren might meet someone who did and repeat the tragedy of Johnnie all over again. I can't allow that to happen. Watching my son die was the hardest thing I've ever had to do. I couldn't do that to anyone else, however indirectly. And I'm too old to adopt, or foster. That means you'd be denying yourself the beauty and privilege of being a parent.' He swallowed hard. 'I can't do that to you, darling.'

She lifted herself up on one elbow and looked down at his, at his face drawn with sorrow and the love that would sacrifice itself for her selfishness — and so needlessly. 'Listen to me, please. I don't *want* to be a parent. The prospect of that responsibility terrifies me, and I know I wouldn't be content to sit at home all day with a baby. I'd go nuts. That's why I've never married. Everyone I've ever been serious about has wanted marriage *and* children, ultimately. I never wanted that before.'

'Before?'

She looked away, but he turned her face back with his hand.

'If we were able to, would you want my children?'

She met his eyes for a long while, then nodded. 'Yes—but because they would be yours, not because they were children. Because I know how much it hurts you not to have children.'

'But I have had a child, and although he's gone, that love, that joy will stay with me forever. And because I've known that love, I can't deny you the opportunity.'

'But I don't want the opportunity, Jack, can't you see that? I would only be doing it for you!'

He met her eyes steadily. 'There's always AID.'

'Artifical insemination by donor?' She gave a short laugh. 'No, thank you. I certainly don't want anybody else's child. Anyway, it's not as if my life is free of children. I'm an aunt nine—nearly ten times over, and we have an endless stream of children through the department. Any frustrated mothering instinct has plenty of scope there.'

'Kathleen, I——'

'Please, Jack. Your love is all I could ever need.'

He searched her face for endless moments, then his eyes filled. 'I give up. Damn it, I don't know why I'm trying to talk you out of it. God knows you're the only thing in my life to have any meaning since Johnnie died. That's why I crawl down holes and chuck myself off cliffs and ride the bike—it's been the only way I could feel alive, but since I met you I've come alive in other ways, ways I'd forgotten long ago. You've taught me to care again, and you've taught me that I matter, that my life is worth something. For a long while I thought it didn't matter if I lived or died, but you've changed all that. I don't have to run any more.'

He sighed and tugged her closer. 'Come here and hold me.'

She snuggled against his side. 'I mean it, Jack,' she said after a moment. 'You're all I need. Perhaps it's greedy to want everything. If I had to choose between having children and having you, it would have to be you. Nothing else could ever matter more.'

'I'm older than you,' he said quietly. 'You could be widowed young, and with no children or grandchildren to fill those lonely years.'

'I could fall under a bus.'

His arms tightened convulsively. 'Don't.'

'You know, with all these tragedies lining up in wait for us, we really shouldn't waste time.'

'Huh? Kath, what — oh, wow. . .'

She giggled. 'What was that again?'

He groaned and laughed. 'Damn it, woman, get up here.'

'Like this?'

He gasped and reached up to her, pulling her down against his chest, and then with a swift movement he turned her beneath him.

'Ooo, fancy stuff!' she teased.

'Be quiet and concentrate.'

'Yes, sir!'

Then there was no more banter, just a ragged silence, broken by sighs and whispers and breathless cries, until at last they lay still again, replete.

After a few minutes Jack groped for the bedside table.

'What are you doing?'

'Getting a cigarette.'

'Oh, no. Put them down.'

'Aw, Kath, come on——'

'No! No, no, no. No! Put them down. Now!'

He sighed heavily and dropped his arm back on the bed. 'You're a cruel woman.'

'Rubbish. Just looking after you.'

'But Confucius he say——'

'Never mind Confucius! I have other plans for you!'

Her hand slid down his ribs, and his eyes widened. 'I'll be exhausted!'

She grinned. 'Mm. Too tired to hold a cigarette.'

He flung his arms wide. 'I'm yours—take me!'

She knelt up beside him and looked down at his body, a satisfied smile on her face. 'You are, too.' Her smile faded, and she levelled her finger at him. 'If I so much as catch you *smiling* at another woman——'

He tugged her down into his arms. 'Don't be silly. If I'm too tired to hold a cigarette I won't be very likely to stray.'

'Hmm. That's true.'

He chuckled. 'Better start now, I've got amazing stamina.'

'The arrogance of the man. Prove it.'

Laughter danced in his eyes. 'My pleasure.'

Hours later he reached for the bedside table again.

'What are you doing?' Kath mumbled drowsily.

'Turning out the light.'

'No cigarette?'

'Uh-uh. I couldn't hold it. You're a wicked, wanton, resourceful woman, Irish.'

She giggled sleepily. 'See? Told you it would work.'

But he was already asleep.

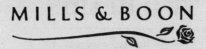

ESCAPE INTO ANOTHER WORLD...

...With Temptation Dreamscape Romances

Two worlds collide in 3 very special Temptation titles, guaranteed to sweep you to the very edge of reality.

The timeless mysteries of reincarnation, telepathy and earthbound spirits clash with the modern lives and passions of ordinary men and women.

Available November 1993   Price £5.55

MILLS & BOON

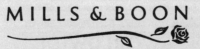

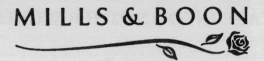

MILLS & BOON